I0692332

Jungle Series

Written By LI DI

Drumming in the Dark Forest

A story about
revenge and growth

Primus Press USA

Original Title: 《黑林鼓声》

Original book by The Writers Publishing House Co.,Ltd.

This edition is published by arrangement with Prunus Press USA, through the agency of China National Publications Import and Export (Group) Co., Ltd.

All rights reserved.

No part of this book may be reproduced, in any form or by any means, without permission in writing from the publisher.

DRUMMING IN THE DARK FOREST

Copyright © Prunus Press USA

Written by Li Di
Translated by Haiwang Yuan
Designed by Brandy Ding

First edition 2022
ISBN: 978-1-61612-144-0

Prunus Press USA

Contents

Chapter 1

A swarthy-faced stout man was drinking silently in the tavern. Grandpa Du Ba sensed murder behind his eyes.

Like a crow's nest perching on a crotch of a tree, Grandpa Du Ba's tavern sat where Mount Beilu and Mount Manuo met the Mengna Forest. Against the rolling mountains and facing the luxuriant, old-growth forest, it was a low-lying stilt bamboo house of the ethnic Aini[1] style. A bit leaning due to the effect of the mountain wind, it was located in the only place where the mountains and the forest could be accessed. A whiff of cooking smoke curled up from among the shadowy wild trees to the tune of red junglefowls' cackles and dholes' howls.

---

[1] Aini is a branch of the Hani ethnic group living in the border area of Yunnan Province, China.

The fog-like cooking smoke wavered like a tavern flag in the wind to attract passer-by guests.

Everyone would climb the wooden staircase to stop for a break in the stilt bamboo house. They could be horse caravan leaders, relative-visiting women, itinerant merchants, or veteran hunters to venture into the valley.

Grandpa Du Ba had already set the oblate, exquisitely pleated bamboo stools for his guests. According to the custom of the ethnic Aini people, such a stool is the symbol of hospitability. In the neatly cleaned tavern, the fire was burning brilliantly in the fire pit, by which were heated beverage and food. They included bitter-tasting *kuding* (liex) infusion; glutinous rice cakes in "white wood" (a tree species in the rutaceae family) steamer that might be gristly but able to stave hunger for a longer time; and stewed meats of wild boar, muntjac, and red deer in an iron pot. A bamboo table was spread with the side dishes of preserved meat of Lady Amherst's pheasants, pickled bamboo shoots and chili peppers, green-cracking russula mushrooms, and Russell's bolete mushrooms.

Grandpa Du Ba also had turbid corn wine that he had brewed himself for guests who were fond of drinking. Consumed too much, it could make a drinker's tongue seize up and legs turn to jelly.

As the bamboo house was just a single-building structure, no guest was allowed to put up for the night on this tavern's bamboo floor polished by footsteps under normal circumstances.

His wife had died early, leaving him no children. As a pebble at the bottom of a river treated passing-by fish as its company, so Grandpa Du Ba welcomed and saw off his passer-by guests. He called a grownup, older or younger than he was "Brother;" a youngster "Son" or "Grandson;" and a skirt-wearing woman with a flower-decorated hairdo "Sister" or "Sister-in-law." He did so as if they were his family members. He might be alone, but he was never lonely. Smiles always played in the clear-cut, crisscrossing furrows on his tanned face weathered like tree bark.

However, a few years ago, a band of bandits led by Wo Guli came to the Mengna Forest. They killed innocent people and seized their properties. Once, to rob merely a fist-size piece of salt, they used leather ropes to strangle five old and young people without batting an eyelid. They then tied rocks to their bodies and, after planting a knife in each of them, dumped them into a pond. The knife wound was meant to release the gas produced from putrefaction that would bloat the body, thus preventing it from floating to the top of the water.

For a time, the pond where muntjacs and red deer had been watering became murky. The "silver-back" vines with purplish blossoms used by sacred langurs as swings were cut off. Even the humid, chilling air in the gloomy old-growth forest reeked of human blood.

Smiles disappeared from Grandpa Du Ba's face.

One day, while chopping wood in the forest, he ran into a pack of dholes. He fired his blunderbuss and dispersed them. He rescued a seven or eight-year-old boy, who had been wounded by a knife but was still alive. He was lying by the side of two bodies. They obviously had died a miserable death because each had a tree stick jabbed to the stomach through the mouth.

"Gosh! The bandits are simply brutes!"

Sighing with sad tears, Grandpa Du Ba carried the boy back to the tavern.

The ill-fated boy was as young as a cucumber not yet shedding the flower from its top. The bamboo-house tavern sheltered him from wind or rain like the leaves of a cucumber plant.

The lonely old man had a companion.

He named the boy Guo Long.

Guo Long called this old man who had saved his life Grandpa.

As a wild loquat on the mountain struggled to thrive in the crack of a rock or a red junglefowl cock down the mountain strove to flourish in wild grass, so Guo Long went through all kinds of adventures with his grandpa in the wooded valley as he grew up. There, they traveled in thistles and thorns, hunted for wild animals, captured rodents and serpents, noodling fish and shrimps, collected mushrooms, and harvested bamboo shoots.

Grandpa Du Ba led the way, and Guo Long followed closely.

One tall and the other short, they braved the wind and rain together.

With one trails of footsteps deep and the other shallow, they waded through mud and water.

By the time a tuff of gray hair stuck out stealthily from grandpa's black-cloth headwear, Guo Long had grown into a sixteen-year-old youngster. He vowed to avenge his ada and ama[2] brutally murdered by the bandits.

He stood as erect as a bamboo stem.

This morning, when the trees were still veiled in fog, Guo Long went to the forest to collect mushrooms, with dewdrops under his feet.

Guo Long had just left for a while when someone knocked at the tavern's bam-boo door.

Bang, bang, bang! Bang, bang, bang!

The banging was very loud.

The reconnaissance company of the bandit-suppressing army had recently entered the area of the Beilu and Manuo mountains. Sensing that their days were numbered, Wo Guli and his bandits escalated their bloody assaults. The people on both sides of the border were scared into hunkering down in their homes. Therefore, the tavern had not been patronized for days.

So, who was knocking at the bamboo door so early in the morning?

Grandpa Du Ba, who was stoking the fire in the fire pit, rose to open the door.

---

[2] Ada and ama means "dad" and "mom" in the Aini dialect.

The bamboo door squeaked open. A swarthy-faced man appeared in front of Grandpa Du Ba.

This man was dressed in authentic Aini costumes: a short top exposing his abdomen, loose pants reaching over his knees, a blue-cloth satchel set with silver sequins being slung across his shoulders, and two rows of silver buckles with carved patterns glistening on his chest.

The dew on his clothes and the mud on his feet betrayed an overnight traveler.

Striding into the tavern with a tailwind, he sat with an imposing bearing at a bamboo table facing the door. He tossed some coins on the table, purchased his wine and meat dish, and started munching and gulping.

In no time, he drank up a whole bamboo tube of wine. But he did not ask for more. With his rough, veined hands, he picked up a piece of boiled muntjac meat dripping with fat, crammed it into his mouth, and champed it without saying a word.

As he chewed vigorously, a long knife scar on his right cheek became prominent.

Although the swarthy-faced man was eating his food quietly, Grandpa Du Ba already detected his intent to kill from his unusual behavior.

This is a man who has killed people before!

From time to time, he trained his sparkling vulture eyes under his black-cloth headwear on the mountain path through the opening of the bamboo door ajar.

Grandpa Du Ba stoked up the fire in the fire pit, singed a small bundle of liex leaves above it, and put it in an earthen bowl. While pouring boiling water into it, he contemplated.

Who's this burly man?

Where did he come from, and where's he going?

Why is he looking at the mountain path from time to time?

Chapter 2

The mountain path.

Both sides were overgrown with waist-deep weeds.

Like a python, it slithered from the mountains into the forest.

The boundless forest was sleeping quietly beneath a thick comforter of a dense fog.

Suddenly a porcupine darted out squealing strangely from the grass. With its quills drooping, it scurried rustling across the fallen leaves and ran for life into the quiet depth of the forest.

Immediately afterward, there came the clear and melodious sound of a horse bell from where the porcupine had been startled.

Two caravan leaders came out of the thick weeds, one after the other. Issuing their voice commands to four horses, they led them toward Grandpa Du Ba's tavern.

The direction from which they came showed that they were from Mount Manuo. They planned to stop at the tavern for a lunch break before resuming their journey to Mount Beilu.

They were men from the Blang ethnic group.

Traveling a long distance with bamboo baskets over their pack saddles, the horses had all worked up a good sweat. A small bundle of tobacco leaves in a basket was revealed when a corner of its dew-covered tarpaulin was brushed up by a tree branch.

The tobacco leaves were professionally cured with glistening golden color.

It was well known that the Blangs hunting with their blunderbusses or crossbows in Mount Manuo could never do without areca nuts and, particularly, tobacco. Even preteens or younger each had a tobacco pipe in their waist.

Every family had a fertile tobacco plot, and every household was expert in curing tobacco.

In fact, the two Blang men were going to the Mengsa Country Fair in Mount Beilu to trade for some glutinous rice and piece goods with the ethnic Dai people from the flatland of the mountainous area.

In the forest, the most hardworking birds are great hornbills that fly back and forth to forage and feed their chicks nestled in tree holes.

In the mountain, the life of the caravan leaders is the toughest as they traverse bumpy roads and brave wind and rain to transport daily necessities.

Now, the two caravan leaders were so tired that they felt weak in their limbs. They sweated profusely, as if they had just been fished out of a water well. Their sweat-soaked clothes clung to their bodies so tightly that they looked like their wrinkled second skin. Their body odor was as stinky as urine.

Fortunately, the sun had not risen. Covered in dew, the grass along the mountain path was still damp, allowing no bit of grass to be swept up by wind. Otherwise, under the scorching sun, awned grass blades flying in the air would cling to the face and tickle. Scratching, however, would cause excruciating pain. Soon, the face would swell like a squash with bumps on the skin. It would be too much to bear.

They saw the tavern's stilt bamboo house presenting itself indistinctly through the foliage of the trees by the roadside in the distance. The man with a full beard shouted to the young man with a high nose bridge and thin eyebrows walking in front of him:

"Hey, Brother Duo Bu, you must be tired, too, eh? How about stopping our horses and taking a break here?"

Patting the lead horse on its rump, Duo Bu said,

"Brother Mang Ga, we'd better not. Our Sai Guo may

have been waiting for us in the tavern for a long time."

"I don't think so." Mang Ga responded with a drawl while shaking his head, "The nocturnal sloth monkeys were still frolicking when we set out. Sai Guo can't make it ahead of us!"

"You know Sai Guo has a hot temper…"

The conversion suddenly stopped.

Duo Bu felt a gust of sinister wind behind him.

He stopped hastily, turned aside, and heard a "swoosh!" A thirty-centimeter-long dagger brushed past his chest like lightning.

If he had not dodged in time, the dagger would have thrusted into his heart from his back.

Duo Bu broke out into a cold sweat!

He screamed:

"Brother Mang Ga!"

The scream was a warning as well as a call for help!

However, the response was a look grimmer than the dagger.

There was no third party on the mountain path overgrown with weeds.

It was Mang Ga who had attempted at Duo Bu's life!

Duo Bu was so shocked that his brain stuttered and his ear rung, as if countless wild bees were buzzing around him.

It was easier to dodge a stealthy attack from behind than to face such an incredible turn of event unfolding before him.

Duo Bu's nimbleness suddenly gave way to sluggishness.

Before he had time to pull his gun out of his waist, Mang Ga had withdrawn the arm he had held out to stab him and, while his arm was still bending, he summoned up all his strength and struck Duo Bu with the elbow.

Before Duo Bu regained his balance, Mang Ga had thrown himself at him.

Bam! The elbow hit Duo Bu right in the pit of his stomach.

The elbow struck like an iron rod and knocked Duo Bu a few steps backwards. He spat a big mouthful of blood and thumped to the ground on his back. His head tilting aside, he went into a coma.

Thinking that he had the upper hand, Mang Ga pounced upon Duo Bu like a tiger, a knife in his hand.

He was going to end Duo Bu's life with a single stab.

Before he got close to Duo Bu, he abruptly froze like a zombie...

He was looking into the dark muzzle of a gun!

It turned out that Duo Bu had pretended that he was unable to withstand the blow. When Mang Ga had hit him in the pit of his stomach with his elbow, he had cut the inside of his cheek by biting and spat a mouthful of blood. Then, the moment he fell, he got his gun ready.

Knowing that he was playing into his opponent's hands, Mang Ga stared into the muzzle dumbfounded, feeling a chill down his spine, and it dispersed all his triumphant fervor.

Suddenly, he cast his dagger into the weeds, and, as if to be pressed by Duo Bu's aggressive glare, he felt his legs give and thumped to the ground on his knees.

"Brother Duo Bu, I'm terribly sorry. Please spare my life, and I'll tell you everything! Everything..."

Duo Bu did not put down his gun. He only tilted it slightly away from Mang Ga's chest.

This minute move did not escape Mang Ga's furtive glance.

Mang Ga sprang up abruptly from his kneeling posture. Grasping Duo Bu's hand holding the gun, he pushed it up so that the gun pointed to the sky. Then, he quickly reached out one of his hands, trying to grab the gun by its grip.

How could Duo Bu allow him to grapple his gun. Clenching his teeth, he balled his left hand in the air into a fist and punched Mang Ga in his right ear.

This blow punctured Mang Ga's eardrum. His eyes went dark and the right side of his head became numb. An excruciating headache immediately followed.

"Ouch!"

With a cry of agony, Mang Ga wobbled, but his hands were still clenching Duo Bu's wrist.

Duo Bu launched another punch in his right ear that was already bleeding. While Mang Ga's face was sent titling, he followed up with a kick in the pit of his stomach.

A kick with the velocity of a few hundred kilograms bashed Mang Ga away from him. He collapsed limply on his back in the weeds.

Giving him no chance to rise on his feet, Duo Bu pulled the trigger and fired.

But it did not fire!

The gun was jammed!

Both were stunned!

Silence reigned all around. Even the weeds stopped waving.

One standing and the other crouching, they were petrified into a fighting sculpture.

Suddenly, Mang Ga sprang up roaring and plunged himself desperately at Duo Bu with his hands open.

Seeing his opponent pouncing on him holding out his hands, Duo Bu kept calm. He held the gun by the barrel, ready to crack Mang Ga's head open with the grip after dodging his lunging attack.

But when he noticed Mang Ga taking something from his sleeve, everything was too late.

Something went into Duo Du. Giving a shudder, he widened his eyes.

The dagger that Mang Ga had cast into the weeds was thrusted into Duo Bu's chest like an ox's horn.

Duo Bu staggered with anguish and collapsed by the feet of Mang Ga.

His legs convulsed a little before he became permanently motionless.

Mang Ga plied Duo Bu's hand open, yanked the gun out, and tucked it into the bosom.

He did not pull the dagger out.

If he had done so, steaming blood would squirt for some distance.

Mang Ga unfastened a leather rope from a horse pack, looped it around the chest of Duo Bu's body, and pulled it behind a horse off the mountain path and into the forest.

He came to a big-leaf tree, broke off a tough, pointed branch, and jabbed Duo Bu's eyes into a pulp.

He was a believer of a popular saying that a murder victim's eyes could capture the image of the perpetrator immediately before his death.

After he finished, Mang Ga carried Duo Bu's body on his back and climbed up the big-leaf tree with tremendous effort.

He pulled the body up and placed it over a big crotch.

This way, it would be hard for passers-by to notice the body. Another benefit was that pythons or leopards, both expert tree climbers, could consume it as a windfall.

Making sure that the body was hung securely, Mang Ga wiped the sweat off his forehead, and clambered down the tree.

His feet had just touched the ground when he heard something stirring behind him. He quickly turned around, only to see two broad swords being swiped at him.

Mang Ga was taken aback. He found it too late to pull

the gun out. Jammed as it was, it would have been useless even if he could have had it available.

The two sword-wielding men were both stalwart with thick brows and ferocious eyes.

As the two broad swords fell upon him from left and right, Mang Ga hit upon an idea in such emergency. He slung the leather rope he had used to tie Duo Bu like a coiling snake and tangled the two swords together.

The blades of the swords crossed each other as the leather rope pulled them together so that their edges were both facing outside. With a kihap-like shout together, the two burly men cut the leather rope off at the same time.

The sections of the leather rope dropped into the thick growth of grass.

But when the two men raised their swords to chop Mang Ga again, he was nowhere to be found.

How could Mang Ga go far?

He was hiding behind the big-leaf tree.

Since he was so close, the two men quickly discovered him.

Wielding their swords, they pounced upon him. Suddenly, Mang Ga roared with alarm and bumped his shoulder against the tree.

The tree shook, and the body placed over its crotch fell cracking down like a boulder.

One of the burly men failed to dodge in time and was rammed to the ground by the body. While he was thumping down, his sword escaped from his hand.

Mang Ga would not give him the time to pick himself up. He sprang from behind the tree to grab the fallen sword.

The other man lunged over and swiped his sword down.

A streak of shining light sent purplish blood splashing. From the air there came a bloodcurdling cry:

"Ouch!"

The burly man looked closely and was stupefied!

In a hurry, he slashed his partner instead of Mang Ga.

Qiao La! Qiao La! …you…you were blind…"

These were the last words of his partner wiggling in a blood pool.

The man named Qiao La flew into a rage. Wielding his broad sword, he threw himself upon Mang Ga.

Mang Ga picked up the other sword from the ground though he was still out of balance. He held it up to parry Qiao La's strike.

He only meant to straighten his back up when the two swords clanked together and ward off his opponent's devastating blow. But when Qiao La lunged forward, he did not strike his sword down like a meteor as Mang Ga had expected. Instead, he suddenly suspended the blade right before it met Mang Ga's. While holding it in midair, he launched a kick as swift as a whirlwind, and it hit Mang Ga right in his tibia bone.

The kick was swift and clean indeed!

It was abrupt, relentless, and accurate.

The tibia bone has the least protection of muscle in a human body. No one, however strong he may be, can sustain such a strike.

With an "Ouch" of agony, Mang Ga leaned aside.

As he leaned, he lost his foothold, and his sword was also off its target.

Qiao La seized the opportunity, and brought his sword down from the midair.

A "swash" followed a "swoosh!"

Half of Mang Ga's head was chopped off.

The flying half of the head fell bloody and mangled in the thicket five or six meters away.

In the thicket, there were two bright eyes.

Chapter 3

They were the eyes of a lanky Aini teen, gleaming like two black grape berries covered in dew.

Hiding in the thicket like a leopard cat, he witnessed this bloody battle that had come so suddenly. He was Guo Long, who was collecting mushrooms.

The drizzle that had fallen at the latter part of the night boosted the growth of the mushrooms in the mist-shrouded forest.

The green brittlegills (russula virescens) with slender white stems popped their heads with greyish green hats from the thick grass under the Homalium cochinchinense trees draped with vines. They were nodding at Guo Long. Silently recoiling under the burflower-tree with penduline tits' nests hanging from it were the seemingly slumbering tawny milkcaps (Lactifluus volemus). With white milky sap oozing out when broken off, this type of mushrooms can be eaten raw. Guo Long picked two, brushed off the dirt from the base of their stems, placed them in his mouth, and munched with heart's content. Fresh and crispy, tawny

milkcaps have a milky taste blended with a subtle sweet flavor. Sheltered under the tri flowers (Trillium govanianum) and playing hide-and-seek with Guo Long were the lurid boletes. They are only edible when cooked. The tri flowers can change colors with varying shades of light: white in the morning, red at noon, and purplish black at dusk. The color of the lurid bolete varies as well. It is yellow when coming out of the soil and turns dark when touched by hand. That is how it has gotten its nickname *jianshouqing* ("black if touched by hand"). This type of mushroom is poisonous if not boiled thoroughly. Standing under the white jade orchid tree, the dark-scaled knights (Tricholoma atrosquamosum) appeared like old men in black cloaks. They seemed to be raising their heads to gaze at the fragrant flowers all over the tree. Guo Long picked some. Meanwhile, his shirts and pants of coarse cloth were fumed with the scent of the orchid tree's flowers. The matsutake mushrooms are the easiest to find because they are always under ubiquitous thick fallen pine needles. The hardest to discover are mushrooms of the termitomyces genus. Tasting like chicken, they are extremely palatable. when you finally locate them, you are not supposed to nip them from the base the way you do with other mushrooms. You must pull them out along with the soil-laden root and wrap them up with big leaves. Otherwise, the fresh flavor would dissipate....

The mushrooms in the forest were as flourishing as the stars in the sky. Fascinated with them, Guo Long picked some here and there, knowing no fatigue. In no time, he had enough to fill a good part of his basket carried on the back.

These mushrooms can be cooked fresh or air-dried so that they could be kept for the consumption by the tavern's guests.

Guo Long found two dew-covered penny bun (Boletus edulis) mushrooms under a tall mountain ebony tree (bauhinia variegate). Their greenish, palm-sized heads curled up slightly. In Guo Long's mind's eye, they suddenly turned into two greenish faces studded with beads of sweat. The wide-open mouth on each face now howled, now wailed. And soon they started fuming. They gurgled and fumed like crabs...

Those were the faces of the tavern's guests, who had eaten the boletus speciosus mushrooms, and its poison was driving them crazy.

That day, Guo Long had picked some boletus speciosus mushrooms, which he mistook for the penny buns (Boletus edulis). He had boiled them and served the dish to two passers-by guests. The guests had just finished a cup of wine when they went crazy, tumbling on the floor crying frantically. Luckily, Grandpa Du Ba came from woodcutting in time. He treated the two guests with an herbal antidote and thus avoided a fatal disaster.

Grandpa Du Ba told Guo Long never to collect boletus speciosus mushrooms. No matter how strong a man was, he would become crazy after eating them, particularly if he ate them with alcohol.

From that day on, Guo Long would uproot any boletus speciosus mushroom that he came across and toss it far away...

It was no exception this time of course.

He pulled the two boletus speciosus mushrooms from the soil and toss them as far as he could.

Like two tiny parachutes, the mushrooms fell into the thick growth of grass.

A horse bell came ding-donging from the fog-clouded mountain path.

The bell sound told him that the horse caravan was heading toward the tavern.

The tavern had had no business for quite a few days. Who were the guys coming through the fog?

Guo Long traced the sound to them.

But when he caught sight of them, he found a caravan leader was already lying on the grassy ground.

Alarmed, Guo Long had hurriedly taken cover in the waist-deep thicket.

Soon, a life-and-death fight had ensued in front of him.

The bloody battle left three ghastly looking bodies lying on their backs or stomachs on the trampled weeds over the muddy ground.

The mountain wind blowing over sent the smell of blood to his nostrils.

Guo Long widened his eyes, lying motionless on his stomach in the thicket.

After killing Mang Ga, Qiao La wiped the blood off his broad sword. Then, he grabbed Mang Ga's body by the shirt and ripped a large piece off it, revealing a swarthy chest.

Guo Long was so stunned that he barely cried out…

A two-headed viper was coiling on Mang Ga's chest.

Guo Long looked closely and found it to be a tattoo!

Qiao La did not seem to pay much attention to the two-headed snake.

He tore open the top, pulled a handgun from Mang Ga's bosom, and tucked it in his own waist.

Afterward, he wiped the sweat off his face, went out of the forest, and went on to the mountain path.

The four horses carrying loads of tobacco stood in the path snorting and nibbled at the tips of young grass on the roadside.

Qiao La walked up to one of the horses. He cut off a rope used to fix the tarpaulin, lifted the tarp up, and revealed the tobacco leaves. Separating the leaves, he pulled a big package wrapped in hay from the bottom of the pack basket.

What's it?

Guo Long gasped at what he saw:

What?!

What Qiao La pulled from the bottom of the tobacco leaves was a bundle of oily shining rifles!

Qiao La immediately dug the weaponry and ammunition from the packs of the other three horses.

There were altogether four bundles of rifles and five boxes of ammunition.

It was too far to see clearly, but Guo Long counted at least thirty rifles in the four bundles.

Qiao La wrapped the rifles and ammunition neatly in a tarpaulin, placed it on a big black horse, and led it down the mountain path into the depth of the forest, with the fallen leaves rustling under his feet.

The foliage finally swallowed Qiao La.

Guo Long knitted his eyebrows into a frown of questions.

Who's this man named Qiao La?

How did he know that there were rifles beneath the tobacco leaves?

Whose rifles are they?

The fog-shrouded mountain and the fields were lying extremely quiet.

Only the beads of dew on the grass blades glittered in the chilling wind suffused with the smell of blood.

Attracted by the smell of the blood, a few crows alighted on the big-leaf tree and fixed their eyes on the three bloody bodies.

A bolder one fluttered down the tree and hopped around the bodies. It seemed too timid to take action lest the dead bodies would spring up alive.

Dead bodies were lying in the wild with crows cawing sadly.

The blood oozing from the bodies gradually turned purple and black.

Who are the murderers and the victims?

Where is Qiao La shipping the rifles and ammunition?

If he's a good man, I should lend him a helping hand.

It would be terrible if he's a bandit.

These rifles and ammunition mustn't fall into the hands of the bandits!

What shall I do?

In the blink of an eye, Guo Long struck on an idea:

I'll shadow him and see where he's going!

Like a lizard catching insects in flight, Guo Long pussy-footed under the cover of the thicket. He followed Qiao La not too far and yet not too close into the dense forest.

The trees covered with vines stood like a huge canopy shielding the forest from light. It might be a hyperbole to say that Guo Long could not see his fingers when held in front of him, but it was indeed very difficult to see anything clearly merely ten feet away. The dried up leaves and twigs fallen on the ground were thick due to years of accumulation and reeked of decomposition. Occasionally, he would step on spots where bubbles were being released under the pressure of his feet!

Leading the horse, Qiao La trudged forward in the old-growth forest.

To prevent the sound of bubbling from alerting Qiao La, Guo Long walked in his footprints where the gas beneath them had already been released. No gas, no bubble, and no sound.

Qiao La walked and walked when he stopped at a tall Malayan yellowwood and looked around. When he was convinced that there was no one watching, he bent over, raked the grass apart with his hands, and, with an effort, suddenly lifted a thick board lid off the soil.

Under the board, there revealed the opening of a dark cave.

What? A cave in the ground here!

It was spacious though not deep.

Guo Long saw Qiao La placing the rifles and ammunition in the cave, put the board lid back, and replaced the turf and pattered it even. He then resumed his journey, leading the horse.

Sizing up the Malayan yellowwood, Guo Long pondered:

Where is Qiao La going after he hid the weaponry here?

Taking a few tawny milkcaps from the basket carried on his back, bound them into a bundle, and fastened it on top of a bush plant.

Viewed afar, it looked as if the bush had produced a few white blossoms.

After marking the location, Guo Long went on shadowing Qiao La.

Qiao La milled around a few times in the forest, tethered the horse to a tropical almond (Terminalia catappa) tree, and plopped down to the ground. He took out a Mauser C96 from his bosom and began to fiddle with it.

Hiding behind a thick burflower-tree, Guo Long fixed his eyes on Qiao La's every move.

After he fixed the gun, Qiao La stood up. Suddenly...

Clucking, clucking, clucking!

Cries of alarm rose behind Guo Long.

Following the cries, there flew up a red junglefowl, which fluttered into the depth of the forest.

It was a hatching hen. A red junglefowl hen does not have fixed locations to hatch their young. It usually pulls some thick fallen leaves apart and sets its nest in the shallow pit. In it, it lays three or five eggs and begins to brood them. Their grayish yellow feathers matched the colors of the fallen leaves so much that no one can detect them even walking up close. Therefore, red junglefowl hens never fly up unless someone step on them.

But Gu Long had been crouching motionless behind the tree. Why had this junglefowl been hen startled and flown up?

From the corners of his eyes, Guo Long caught sight of a greater green snake. Opening its mouth wide, it was trying to gulp down an egg.

I see! The red junglefowl hen was startled by this greater green snake!

Qiao La waded through the fallen leaves, walking rust-ling, rustling over to the burflower-tree.

His Mauser C96 was always pointing at the tree.

Yikes! I can't hide anymore!

I'll come out and tell him I'm collecting mushrooms here in the old forest.

No, it's too late. He won't believe me.

What shall I do?

Turning his face aside, Guo Long saw...

...the greater green snake that had startled the red

junglefowl hen was still gobbling up the eggs.

It seemed that it had set its mind on devouring all he eggs in the nest.

The site of the greedy greater green snake gave Guo Long an idea!

With his hands open, he threw himself upon the snake. Gripping it by the neck with one hand and holding its tail with the other, he abruptly pulled the snake up.

It was a quick and clean move!

With an egg in its mouth, the greater green snake could not bite Guo Long.

He had learned from Grandpa Du Ba this unique skill of catching snakes quickly without making a slip of his hand.

When Guo Long just had the snake in his grip, Qiao La had reached the left side of the burflower-tree.

Guo Long quickly ducked, bent himself into a ball, and sneaked to the right side of the tree swiftly. Then, he let go the snake on the left.

The greater green snake slithered out of the grass toward Qiao La.

Qiao La was taken aback and hastily slid his legs apart.

The greater green snake slid away between his legs, still holding an egg in its mouth!

Realizing what had startled the red junglefowl, Qiao La stopped.

He never imagined that another "red junglefowl" was still behind the burflower-tree. He was there because he had

had no time to flee.

Qiao La returned to the tropical almond tree and gave the rein a pull to make sure that the horse was securely tethered to the tree. Then, he walked away toward the depth of the forest.

What? He's left his horse behind?

How dangerous it is to park a horse here with so many beasts of prey lurking in the forest!

From this single act, Guo Long concluded that Qiao La was by no means a good man.

He followed Qiao La for a while and found him heading to the tavern in a round-about way.

I'll outstrip him and get to the tavern first. I'll tell my grandpa everything so that he can be prepared.

Having made up his mind, Guo Long turned to a narrow winding trail trampled out by muntjacs. It could lead him back to the tavern.

He trotted and trotted, and in no time, he had covered quite a distance.

Before Guo Long came out of the forest, two other burly men entered the tavern.

Chapter 4

The two burly men were dressed in the Aini costumes.

The one walking in the front had a broad face with a full beard. Feeling hot from a long journey, he had his shirt unbuttoned, revealing his swarthy sinewy chest.

Pushing the squeaky bamboo door open, he quickly scanned every cranny and nook of the room with his spark-ling eyes.

The one following the broad-faced man closely did not look benign at all. His eyes were as round as those of a mad bull. His mouth was as wide as

that of a frog, from which his front teeth vied with one another in jutting out. His gnarled face, as cold as ice, could probably never break into a smile. Such a face gave the impression that he was a man that could kill a man without batting his eyelid.

Carrying nothing at all, the two burly men entered the tavern barehanded one after the other.

Although he saw the two men coming in, the swarthy-faced man sitting opposite the door did not even lift his eyelids. He was still munching his meat dish. The rich and greasy muntjac meat was so well-done that as he tore a piece apart and crammed it in his mouth, it broke up with little chewing effort.

As soon as he saw the newcomers, Grandpa Du Ba rose and went up to greet them while wiping his hands on the front of his top.

As he looked into the eyes of the man coming in first, Grandpa Du Ba twitched his eyebrow.

It's he?

It can't be…

Meanwhile, Grandpa Du Ba extended his welcomed to the guests:

"Hey, you must be tired after your long journey. Please be seated in here. What would you like to eat?"

At the same time, he stole a glance at the broad-faced man.

Yes, it's him! There's no mistake!

What's he here for…?

"A bowl of tea first, please!" said Broad Face.

As he placed his order, Broad Face looked into Grandpa Du Ba's eyes. However, his face remained as expressionless as he first came in.

During their conversation, Grandpa Du Ba blocked the view of the swarthy-faced man munching his meat dish quietly.

Taking advantage of this blockage, Swarthy Face took a sidelong glance at the two new arrivals in the small mirror hung on the bamboo-fence wall.

Obviously, he had found this palm-sized mirror useful when he had first come in and sat down in the tavern.

One glance was enough to give him confidence.

Grandpa Du Ba came to the fire pit, took the flame-licked, oblate earthen pot off the hook at the end of a chain hanging down from the beam of the bamboo house. He poured the boiling water from it into two cups with tea leaves in them. He then served the piping-hot tea to the two new guests while asking them to be seated.

Square Face sat down with his back to the fire pit and opposite the swarthy-faced man.

He held the bowl of tea to his mouth and blew the tea leaves aside gently. But he glanced sideways at the swarthy-faced man behind the rising steam from the tea.

Swarthy Face ate up all his muntjac meat dish, wiped his mouth, and nodded at Grandpa Du Ba, meaning to say goodbye.

He then stepped out of the tavern.

Square Face followed Swarthy Face with his eyes. He moved his lips a bit but did not say anything.

The man with bulging eyes and a wide-opening mouth looked sullen and looked at nobody.

Exchange of greetings among the guests was normal although they were strangers.

Being so quiet indicated that both parties were unusual.

Seeing the previous guest leaving, Grandpa Du Ba was about to strike up a conversation with Square Face when the sound of metal hitting metal drifted into the tavern:

Ding-dong, ding-dong, ding-dong...

A horse bell!

The two burly men put their tea bowls down at the same time.

Ding-dong, ding-dong, ding-dong...

The sound of the horse bell was coming toward the tavern!

The two burly men looked briefly at each other before they stormed out of the tavern, with Bulging Eyes following Square Face.

The ding-dong of the horse bell came from the bushes.

It sounded that the caravan was still bumping along on the forest path covered in fallen leaves.

The two burly men followed the mountain path into the dense forest.

They were walking swiftly when there came a rustle from the thicket. Before he could give a cry, Bulging Eyes' neck was held fast by an arm.

He writhed with great effort trying to look back. He was startled when he got a chance!

He could not believe that what he saw was a face.

Because there had never been such a terrifying face in the world!

It was a blank one, with neither nose nor mouth. Where the eyes should have been there were two dark holes, from which a murderous beam shot out!

Just as when the face appeared, a chillingly sharp dagger was dug into the chest of Bulging Eyes.

Sensing a stir behind him, Square Face quickly pulled his gun out from his waist.

He was so nimble that when he got hold of the gun, he had already loaded it.

But it was an act after he heard the stir after all!

And the action came after what had already happened.

Therefore, it was a step too late.

"Put your gun down! Or I'll stab him!"

The overbearing demand flew over like a rock and stopped up Square Face's muzzle.

He saw clearly that the man who came out of the blue to hold his partner under the threat of a dagger was wearing a red-cloth hood.

Square Face faltered.

"Did you hear me? Put your gun down!" the hooded man demanded sternly.

While his partner's life was hanging in the balance at the tip of his dagger, a wrong move would cause blood to shed.

Flop!

Square Face cast his gun onto the grassy ground.

"Turn around! Hands up!" yelled the hooded man.

He was really a seasoned robber!

Without his gun, Square Face was already on the defensive. Turning around with hands up, he was in an even more unfavorable situation.

Before turning around, Square Face took a hard look at the hooded man.

The hood might shield his features, but the blank face still told Square Face that he was a savage.

There was no way to reason with him. Nor was there room for negotiation. There was only one option:

Killing him or being killed!

In a situation like this, to kill him, he needed to make temporary concessions in order to seek an opportunity to turn the tables.

Suppressing his anger, Square Face raised his hands and

turned around slowly.

Now, he wished that the horse bell would sound near him.

Strangely, the sound of the horse bell had completely died out.

Silence reigned in the mountain and the fields.

There was no time for thinking. Square Face knew that the hooded man would approach him soon.

No, he was aiming for the gun on the grassy ground.

The gun would assure his success.

To turn the tables, the only chance was when he stooped to pick up the gun.

Just then, Square Face heard something stirring behind him.

Shuffling, shuffling, shuffling!

Digging his dagger into the back of his hostage, the hooded man was inching forward...

To kill!

Or to be killed!

Now it was time!

The hooded man was to pick up the gun while Square Face was to fight back. Just at this extremely critical moment, Bulging Eyes suddenly kicked the gun about a dozen meters away.

However, this move came at the price of his life.

The relentless hooded man let out a strange cry and raised his dagger...

Square Face tried to grab it.

But it was too late.

Instantly a forty-meter-long dagger was pushed into the chest of Bulging Eyes, leaving only the handle outside.

What a ruthless stab!

Without even giving a whimper, a man as tough as led instantly gave up the ghost, his swarthy face turning as pale as frost.

Square Face flew into a rage, his eyes bloodshot.

He punched the hooded man on his face with both hands

He had invested all his hatred and strength in his fists.

The hooded man remained unperturbed. He pulled the dagger out abruptly from Bulging Eyes. Blood jetted out and splashed Square Face.

Square Face was suddenly covered with blood!

Blinded by the blood, he could see nothing but red in front of his eyes.

He hastily reached his hand to wipe the blood off, only to see a dazzling light looming in the red. He dodged swiftly and heard a whoosh passing by. The hooded man's dagger missed him. Before he could withdraw the dagger, Square Face had gripped the wrist of his dagger-holding hand with his as strong as eagle claws. And, taking advantage of the momentum, Square Face pulled the hooded man's arm so hard that, with a "crack," it came off its joint.

With a bloodcurdling cry, the hooded man dropped his dagger.

Getting the upper hand, Square Face was not eager to pick up the gun. Instead, he launched a salvo of swift punches and smashed the hooded man to a pulp. While spitting blood, the latter retreated successively in defeat. Square Face lunged forward and, with a kick, sent him flying like a strayed kite into a good distance.

The hooded man rolled and crawled for a while without being able to struggle up.

Square Face stepped quickly forward and was about to end his life when someone in the thicket shouted,

"A hidden weapon!"

Before the shout died out, the hooded man on the ground flicked his hand. A streak of light like a dragonfly flew straight toward Square Face…

A flying lancet!

Seeing his opponent launching a hidden weapon, Square Face was startled. He turned swiftly.

But it was too late to dodge. He turned his chest away in time but not his right arm.

Meanwhile, "Swoosh!"

A hunting javelin flew out of the thicket.

It fleeted with wind and a chilling glint. It hit the hooded man right at the center of his back.

It was a bulls 'eye!

With a cry of anguish, the hooded man backed a few steps and fell on his back.

As he fell, he carried the javelin on his back and pushed the other end on the ground with the full weight of his body. The sharp head pierced through his chest and sent his blood squirting like a fountain.

The javelin head had lifted the shirt, revealing a double-headed snake tattoo on the chest!

While the hooded man fell, a clear, melodious sound of a horse bell came from the thicket nearby.

Ding-dong!

Square Face was curious.

But he had no time to look for his savior. He went up to the thicket and craned his neck to look, only to see a coir rope pressed beneath the back of the hooded man.

Square Face tugged at the coir rope, and the horse bell started sounding in the nearby thicket.

Ding-dong! Ding-dong!

I see!

Square Face was vexed. He hauled at the coir rope and broke it. He then pulled the hood off the man's head…

Gosh! It was Swarthy Face, the man eating silently in the tavern.

And the one who saved his life with the javelin was none other than Grandpa Du Ba, the owner of the tavern.

Seeing Grandpa Du Ba coming out of the thicket, Square Face was about to say something, when all of a sudden, he shivered all over, and thump! He collapsed to the ground like felled tree.

Grandpa Du Ba paled with shock. He stepped forward swiftly, scooped his upper body up and held him in his arms. He cried out repeatedly:

"Sai Guo! Sai Guo…!"

Square Face opened his eyes with difficulty, his otherwise sparkling eyes already tarnished.

"Grandpa Du Ba…"

"Sai Guo! Sai Guo!" Grandpa Du Ba's hands trembled.

His experience told him that the man in his arms was breathing his last breath. "Sai Guo, grandpa knew you were the ethnic Blang hero from the Mengda Village of Mount Beilu. When I saw you come in dressed like a Aini man today, I figured out you must have come about an important matter…"

Sai Guo did not have much time for Grandpa Du Ba to go on. Shaking Grandpa Du Ba's arm repeatedly, he said.

"Hurry! Hurry! Zha Geli is coming to the tavern to get the rifles. Go and intercept him on his way… Tell him…tell him…"

Without finishing, he gasped his last.

He gave up his life.

Not before he left these words of great importance.

Mother Earth was quiet.

She had nurtured a life with great care and now accepted the death in silence.

Grandpa Du Ba's glassy eyes fell upon Sai Guo's right arm.

His brawny arm was bitten by a lancet as if by a bug.

How could the life of such a robust man taken by a knife less than ten centime-ters long?

Because it had been laced with the "death upon touch" poison!

The "death upon touch" is the local nickname for the antiaris toxicaria tree that produces purple blossoms and berries. Milky sap oozing from its branches and leaves contain rank poison. A knife laced with it kills its victim by coagulating his blood upon coming into contact.

With teary eyes, Grandpa Du Ba held Sai Guo with both arms and laid his body on the ground with great care.

"Oh Sai Guo, you were already an eagle of the Blang people in life able to fly over mountains and through woods. But you're tired with flying. Pull back your wings and find a peaceful place to have a good rest…"

Grandpa Du Ba was murmuring when he remembered Sai Guo's last words. He became so anxious that he felt his heart skip a beat.

"Hurry! Hurry! Zha Geli is coming to the tavern to get the rifles. Go and intercept him on his way… Tell him…tell him…"

Grandpa Du Ba knew Zha Geli as much as he knew Sai Guo. He compared Sai Guo to an eagle of the Blangs and Zha Geli to a tiger of the Aini people.

Zha Geli was a well-known hunter of remarkable skills from the ethnic Aini's Galuo Village on Mount Beilu.

Ten days ago, Qi Su, commander of the reconnaissance company of the bandit-suppressing troops of the PLA, led an enforced squad into Galuo Village from the Blang's Mengda Village. In Galuo Village, the squad established an army-civilian joint defense team. The villagers elected Zha Geli the team leader. He had come to the tavern twice in the guise of an Aini man to learn about the bandit activities from Grandpa Du Ba. From Qi Su's firm voice, Grandpa Du Ba could tell that the days of the bandits were numbered. He hoped that Zha Geli could stop by his tavern often.

But, now, Sai Guo's last words that Zha Geli was on his way to his tavern made Grandpa Du Ba's heart skip a beat!

At such an unusual moment, Zha Geli's arrival must be unusual as well!

Although the hooded man has died, the tavern is still besieged by an invisible danger.

Invisible dangers are real dangers.

I must go to intercept Zha Geli and tell him everything about what has happened here.

Zha Geli, where are you now?

Chapter 5

Zha Geli had already come to the foot of Mount Beilu.

When he had left Galuo Village, the row after row of stilt bamboo houses shielded by the beautiful windmill palms and the lush areca palms were still slumbering quietly in the dense fog.

Now, when he looked back from afar, he saw the fog over the mountain already dissipated, with millions of sunrays caressing lovingly the grass and trees swayed by the mor-ning breeze.

Galuo Village sitting halfway on the mountainside were hidden in the luxuriant green. However, the "Crow Tree" standing as massive as a grove itself in front of the village could still be seen clearly.

The "Crow Tree" was, in fact, a banyan tree with overg-rown foliage. Its trunk was so thick that it was hard for four or five people to wrap around it hand in hand. Its silver-grey boughs extended to the blue sky. From those boughs grew many dark-green aerial roots. Some of them went straight into the earth and grew up as trees, and others were hanging in the midair swaying in the wind, using the air dampened by the pluvial weather as the soil from which they absorbed their nutrients. There-

fore, a tree begot trees and roots gave birth to roots, and eventually it grew into an exuberant "grove."

A tree-turned "grove!"

A marvel was already spectacular, but there was something more spectacular in this marvel.

There were countless crow nests on the dense boughs and branches covering an area of sixty square meters. The crows, totaling about a thousand, had been multiplying generation after generation. The number of the nests increased with the growth of this banyan tree. They normally enjoyed a peaceful life. But when they were startled, they would, in the blink of an eye…

…flow up together to block a large part of the sky.

They cawed together, and their chorus reached far and wide.

It would make a resplendent sight.

And the caws lingered for a long time.

That was why the Aini residents of Galuo Village called this huge banyan the "Crow Tree."

The "Crow Tree" was respected as sacred by the residents of Galuo Village.

Legend had it that the ancestor of Galuo Village had built the first stilt bamboo house on the side of Mount Beilu. It was, at the time, overgrown with thistles and thorns and teeming with beasts of prey. As soon as he finished building the house, a crow alighted on the roof holding a tree seed in its mouth.

After so many years and generations, the Aini people in Galuo Village had survived with tenacity like this first crow.

Their faces were as dark as cow dung;

Their hands were as dry as tree bark;

Their feet were as tough as horse hooves.

Regardless of seasons and occasions, all of them, men and women, wore only a palm-sized piece of animal hide to cover their private parts. Other than that, they had not even a rag.

When the cogon grass grew longer on the mountaintop, they climbed up on all fours, cut it, and brought it back to roof the gamble roof of their stilt bamboo houses. When gusts of violent wind swept the roof off their stilt bamboo house at a rainy midnight filled with the howls of wolves and roars of tigers, the whole family would crouch around the fire pit to shield it from the rain with their bare backs. They did this to prevent the fire from being doused. When cock-a-doodle-doos ushered in the dawn, the villagers would kowtow to A'ao'abo, a god that they believed to be governing everything on the Earth. They would pray for good harvests. Afterward, they would climb over a few hills and set a big fire to burn a large tract of woods down. Then, they would poke holes in the soil covered with ashes and place seeds of cereal crops in them…

They had struggled!

They had survived!

They had survived chilly wind and cold wind as well as the jaws of tigers and wolves.

They had suffered all the miseries of human history in the world.

Who would have expected that, after they had gone through so many trials and tribulations, they were hit by a band of hideous bandits who killed without batting an eyelid? Worse than beasts of prey, they simply denied them the right to survive.

How could the villagers survive without wiping out these vermin-like bandits?

So, they were determined to unite as one in the fight against them!

Just at the critical moment, the reconnaissance company of the PLA's bandit-suppressing troops came to Galuo Village.

They gave the Aini villagers hope.

The Mengda and Galuo villages guarded the pass of Mount Beilu from left and right. Although they each had an army-civilian joint defense team established one after another, they were poorly armed: Apart from about ten rifles and handguns, what they had available were only their blunderbusses and crossbows for hunting. To arm the army-civilian joint defense teams so that they could help the PLA troops to suppress the bandits, the district government in Mount Manuo decided to allot thirty-two rifles and five boxes of ammunition to the villages of Galuo and Mengda.

Militiamen Duo Bu and Mang Ga from the Mengda Village had been dispatched to pick up the rifles and ammunition three days ago.

Zha Geli's mission was to meet the two militiamen and

get the weaponry allotted to Galuo Village from them.

The place to meet was Grandpa Du Ba's tavern.

Before his departure, Company Commander Qi Su put a Mauser C96 in Zha Geli's waistband and advised him to be cautious.

Uncle Yue Mo, deputy leader of the army-civilian joint defense team, suggested dispatching two more militiamen to go with him. But Zha Geli said, "You'll be very busy when the main body of the bandit-suppressing troops arrives at our village ahead of schedule. So, I'd better go myself. I'll return before sunset. Don't worry about me!"

Patting him on his shoulder, Uncle Yue Mo said, "Alright, you don't have to worry about us here, either! I heard that Sai Guo, leader of the army-civilian joint defense team of Mengda Village, is also on his way to meet Duo Bu and Mang Ga.

"Really?" Zha Geli smiled, "As I've been busy, I haven't seen him for a long time. It's great I'll have a chance to meet him!"

This had been how Zha Geli left the village.

"Cock-a-doodle-doo!"

"Cock-a-doodle-doo!"

The crows of red junglefowls came from thick grass.

Zha Geli strode into the valley of Mount Beilu.

This swarthy, lanky man of medium stature was in his late thirties. He had thick eyebrows shaped like swords above his eyes as bright as fire. He had an angular nose with a high bridge. He was wearing clothes of homespun cloth of the indigo color. His loose pants with the cuffs above his ankles swept the dew-covered grass as he walked. The sun gave his long, sunken-cheeked face a dark tan typical of an Aini man living at a high altitude.

He walked swiftly to the valley of Mount Beilu, scanning the crag walls on both sides overgrown with bushes.

Suddenly, Company Commander Qi's words rang in his ears:

"This batch of weaponry allotted by the district comes just in time! The main force of the bandit-suppressing troops has well recuperated from previous battles north of Mount Manuo and will come to the Galuo and Mengda villages this afternoon ahead of time. A big army-civilian joint campaign to suppress the Wo Guli's bandits will soon begin. The battle north of Mount Manuo was extremely fierce. Entrenched in the old-growth forest, Brother Long's bandits were in the dark while the PLA troops were in the open. As a result, while our troops suffered heavy casualties, Brother Long and some of the bandits slipped out of the siege. We must learn the lesson from the Mount Manuo battle. We must stamp out Wo Guli's bandits after luring them out of the Mengna Forest by all means!"

The reminiscence of Company Commander Qi Su's words gave him an idea:

Well, how wonderful it will be to lure Wo Guli's bandits out of the Mengna Forest to the valley of Mount Beilu so that we can ambush them as soon as they come out and cut off their route of retreat before wiping them out!

But how to lure Wo Guli's bandits out of the forest?

Zha Geli was lost in thinking when "whiz!" there flew a sharp arrow from the thicket by the path.

The arrow went straight toward Zha Geli.

Before he had time to dodge, it went into his chest.

"Ouch…!"

Zha Geli gave a bloodcurdling scream.

With the scream, Zha Geli backed a few steps holding the arrow stuck in his chest. He fell thumping to the ground. His body stiffened after he kicked a few times.

Seeing Zha Geli fell with the arrow, a hunchback came out of the thicket.

This man had a face shaped like a bottle gourd, and his eyes glowed like those of a leopard.

Though hunchbacked, he was still pretty nimble.

He went up to Zha Geli, bent over, and reached his hand to get his handgun from his bosom.

Before the hunchback touched the grip of his gun, Zha Geli surprised him by punched him in the cheek with the hand that had been holding the arrow. The punch sent the hunchback staggering a few steps back.

Zha Geli instantly flipped up like a fish and stood on his feet.

"Augh!'

The hunchback turned to run, thinking of Zha Geli as a haunting zombie.

Zha Geli was no zombie at all.

He was not dead!

When the arrow had flown over, the quick-eyed Zha Geli nimbly grasped it. At the same time, he held it against his chest and fell screaming, giving his opponent the impression that he was hit.

By pretending to be dead, he not only avoided the hidden attack but also turned the tables.

How could Zha Geli allow the hunchback to run away?

He pulled his gun out, clocked the hammer, and shouted "Stop!"

The hunchback was still running.

"If you don't stop, I'll fire and kill you!"

The hunchback would not stop.

I must catch him alive, so I can't shoot to kill him.

Zha Geli pressed his finger on the trigger, ready to shoot the hunchback in his leg.

But he stopped short of pulling it.

He was aware that he had just learned how to shoot a gun ten days before. He was not certain if he could hit the target at which he pointed his gun. *What if I miss his leg and shoot him in the head? Then I'll lose a potential source of the information I need.*

No, I can't shoot!

Zha Geli tucked the gun in his bosom and sprang to catch up with him, extending his arms like a flying eagle.

He was carried by a pair of legs capable of chasing deer. He ran so fast that wind whistled by his ears.

He had almost gained upon the hunchback, when suddenly...

...the latter turned around with a glistening dagger in his hand. He threw himself upon Zha Geli and stabbed him!

The stab was so swift and violent that it hit Zha Geli running up in the chest. Clank! It struck a metal, which was the handgun in his bosom.

It was a close call!

If it were not for the wooden grip of the gun, the stab would cut through Zha Geli's abdomen.

When the tip of the dagger hit the metal screw on the wooden grip with a clank, the opponents were glaring into each other's eyes, both ablaze with extreme enmity!

Zha Geli instantly recognized the hunchback as La Bendu, a caravan leader from his village.

That's odd!

We had no grievances against each other. Why did he plot to kill me?

Not giving him time to find an answer, La Bendu pounced on him again, dagger in hand.

Turning sideways, Zha Geli dodged the attack.

At the moment, they were facing each other from north to south.

Zha Geli glared at his opponent as a tiger eyed its prey as he kept moving his feet.

His move seemed to be involuntary, but in fact, he was doing so to position himself with his back to the west.

Unaware of Zha Geli's trick, La Bendu thought of him as trying to grab the dagger. So, he moved his feet accordingly so that he could face Zha Geli all the time.

Zha Geli gained his foothold facing the west this way. By then, La Bendu had been in a position where he was facing the east.

Suddenly, his eyes were blinded by the sun that had just risen.

He squinted instinctively.

Just then, Zha Geli roared, reached out as if to grab the dagger from La Bendu.

Already dazzled by the sun, La Bendu did not see Zha Geli's move clearly. Assuming that Zha Geli was lunging forward baring his chest, La Bendu made a desperate decision. Clenching his teeth, he pounced at Zha Geli, attempting to thrust his dagger into his chest.

He had never expected Zha Geli to feint the attempt to grab his dagger.

As La Bendu thrusted his dagger forward and Zha Geli tilted his upper body to the left, the dagger was now in the gap under Zha Geli's right arm. Before La Bendu had a chance to withdrew it, Zha Geli pressed his right arm down hard and pinned La Bendu's dagger-holding hand against his side. Zha Geli then reached his left hand out swiftly and seized La Bendu by his throat.

La Bendu started rolling his eyes before Zha Geli exerted any strength.

Short of breath, he felt as if all his limbs were out of joint.

Zha Geli quickly twisted La Bendu's arm over and disarmed him of his dagger. He followed up with a kick in his bottom and knocked him to the ground on his face. Then he lost no time in treading him on his back.

Knowing his deadly strength as a martial arts trainee, Zha Geli did not tread too hard. Otherwise he would have broken his backbone and punctured his lungs, thus squeezing his blood out of his mouth and nostrils. La Bendu felt his "gentle" stamp weighing as heavy as a slab of five hundred kilograms. He found it difficult to breathe.

"Ouch! Aw…aw…"

La Bendu was moaning.

The edge of a chilling dagger was suddenly pressed between two of La Bendu's neck bones.

And Zha Geli's questions proved more chilling than the dagger:

"Tell me why you are trying to kill me!"

La Bendu stopped moaning. He bit his lip as his bottle-gourd-shaped face was pressed on the ground.

"You're clamming up, aren't you? Aright, I'll start dismembering you from here!"

As he said so, Zha Geli put some pressure on the dagger. La Bendu gave a bloodcurdling scream, and blood oozed from the back of his neck.

"I'll tell you. I'll tell you...!"

La Bendu cried out.

"Good, go ahead! Why're you trying to kill me?"

"...he, he said you were going to get the rifles and demanded that I kill you on your way..."

"He? Who's he?"

"I don't know..."

"Well?"

"I really don't know!"

"Then, how did he tell you what to do?"

"He...he carved his direction on a bamboo slip and placed it in a bamboo basket I had placed outside my stilt bamboo house. This was how he made me do things each time."

Zha Geli thought for a while before he continued,

"What else did he ask you to do besides killing me?"

"He also asked me to go to Grandpa Du Ba's tavern..."

"To do what?"

"To deliver...deliver a letter..."

"To deliver a letter?"

"Yes."

"To whom?"

"To Wo Guli..."

"Where's the letter?"

"It's in...in my headwear..."

Zha Geli pulled the headwear off La Bendu's head and unfurled it. Sure enough, a small bamboo slip dropped out.

The inscription read:

Don't attack Galuo tomorrow morning

Gosh, even La Bendu also works for Wo Guli!

Suppressing his anger, Zha Geli went on questioning him, "Whom will you hand the letter to after you get to the tavern?"

"No one. I'll just place it in the hole in the Chinese honey locust (Gleditsia sinensis) tree outside the tavern. Someone from the forest will come to get it."

"You mean Wo Guli planned to attack Galuo Village tomorrow morning, don't you?"

"Yes, yes! He feared that after gaining its foothold in Galuo Village, the PLA main force would block his way to get out of the mountain. He wants to take Galuo and burn it down before the joint defense team gets their weapons and the PLA main force arrives…"

"What else can you tell me?"

"Here's more. Yesterday, I received a secret letter sent out from the forest. The letter orders me to place a piece of charcoal in the tree hole today if the situation remains the same and warrants an attack against Galuo Village."

It is the Aini people's hereditary custom to use sugar cane as a message of friendship and charcoal a message of war."

The person behind La Bendu made him deliver a secret letter instead of charcoal. Obviously, he had learned that the bandit-suppressing main force would arrive at Galuo Village ahead of schedule.

An ingenious stratagem suddenly struck Zha Geli like a

lightning.

It was to beat the bandits at their own game. He would place a piece of charcoal in the tree hole so that the Wo Guli bandits would act upon their original plan to attack Galuo Village tomorrow morning. At the same time, he would alert the PLA bandit-suppressing troops so that they could lie in wait on both sides of the Mount Beilu Valley tonight!

If what La Bendu had told him was true, the stratagem would lead to the annihilation of the Wo Guli bandits.

Zha Geli decided to go to the tavern, place a piece of charcoal in the tree hole, and then come back to deal with La Bendu.

"You have to put up with this. Get up! Unfasten your waistband!"

Zha Geli was going to tie La Bendu to a tree in the forest.

La Bendu stood up trembling. His shivering hands reached to his waistband.

Seeing that La Bendu was going to unfasten his waistband, Zha Geli tucked his handgun in his bosom.

Suddenly, La Bendu, who pretended to unfasten his waistband, threw himself like a tiger upon Zha Geli and seized the gun in Zha Geli's bosom.

Before La Bendu leveled the gun, Zha Geli roared,

"There're no bullets in it!"

La Bendu was stunned.

The brief pause gave Zha Geli the opportunity to lunge forward. He quickly grabbed La Bendu by the hand holding the gun and pressed it downward with all his strength.

La Bendu tried all he could to point the gun up.

During the tussle, La Bendu accidentally fired the loaded gun. And the muzzle happened to be dug into his own forehead.

Band!

His head popped, scattering red blood and white brains at once.

La Bendu killed himself.

Zha Geli heaved a sigh of relief. He dragged the body into the forest by the path.

After he concealed the body, he came out, only to see a man standing before him like a tower.

It was none other than Grandpa Du Ba.

Grandpa Du Ba pulled Zha Geli into his arms. With his quivering hands, he kept shaking Zha Geli by his shoulders.

He told Zha Geli about the death of Sai Guo.

Before he finished, tears trickled from his eyes…

Zha Geli realized instantly that he would have to shoulder more responsibilities.

Controlling his grief, he went back to the tavern with Grandpa Du Ba, helping him by the arm.

The tavern was empty, cheerless, and dreary.

Zha Geli asked, "Where's Guo Long?"

Grandpa Du Ba responded, "He went out to collect mushrooms in the early morning. He should've returned by now."

He had just finished when Guo Long threw himself into the tavern, screaming, "…hurry, hurry! Rifles, rifles! Someone called Qiao La…"

Chapter 6

Qiao La trekked in the dense forest. The further he walked, the fewer the trees he saw and the thicker the bushes became.

Looking up at the mountainside not far away, he caught sight of a corner of a stilt bamboo house, the seat of Grandpa Du Ba's tavern. It popped out of a lush hardy banana and mul-berry groves.

Qiao La was sweating all over after a long journey in the forest. Normally, he should have gone to the tavern to refresh himself with some food and drink.

But, on the contrary, when he saw the tavern, he stooped down and hid himself cautiously in the thicket. He crawled forward trying to avoid being seen through the rear windows of the guest rooms.

What was he up to by being so furtive?

A Chinese honey locust tree stooped silently on the mountain path near the tavern, its thick foliage casting a shadow on the grass.

It was this Chinese honey locust tree that Qiao La was looking for.

He sneaked to the tree, glanced at the tavern sideways, and made sure that nothing was stirring. He surveyed the surroundings and found no one walking about. He then reached his hand slowly into the thick grass under the tree.

There was a tree hole beneath the grass.

Qiao La fumbled in the tree hole.

Suddenly, his shoulders jerked, as if his hand touched a snake.

There was no snake in the tree hole.

He felt a piece of charcoal.

A piece of charcoal that indicated a warrant for an attack against Galuo Village tomorrow morning.

Qiao La instantly saw with his minds' eye a scene of flames lighting up the sky and people crying and dogs barking...

All the images that could arouse his beastly instinct flashed frame by frame. He could not help breaking into a sinister laughter.

Of course, he was not aware of three pairs of eyes were being fixed upon his every move.

They were the eyes of Zha Geli, Grandpa Du Ba, and Guo Long, who had been waiting for his arrival under the cover of the hard banana grove for a long time.

Watching the charcoal that he had placed in the tree hole taken away by Qiao La, Zha Geli whispered to Grandpa Du Ba and Guo Long hiding by his side, "Now, we've got some solid clues. Qiao La and the guy who had been killed were all members of the Wo Guli's band. Their purpose of getting out of the forest was twofold: to intercept the rifles and to get the secret message. The information about the transfer of the rifles at the tavern this morning had been reported to Wo Guli by a mole hiding in Galuo Village. But Qiao La had not expected that Mang Ga suddenly killed Duo Bu on their way with the purpose of having the rifles transported under their escort all to himself..."

Guo Long could not help cutting in, "Was Mang Ga a militiaman from the Mengda Village?"

"Yes, he had wormed his way into the militia. He had a tattoo of two-headed snake. He and the swarthy-faced man that had first arrived in the tavern belonged to the same band. The swarthy-faced man recognized Sai Guo and killed him."

"It was like two leopards grabbing the same Himalayan blue sheep!" said Grandpa Du Ba. "It seems that Mang Ga and the swarthy-faced man were from a different band of bandits, different from the Wo Guli band!"

Knitting his eyebrows, Zha Geli said, "Yes, they were mostly likely from Brother Long's band!"

"Brother Long's band of bandits?" Guo Long widened his eyes alarmed, "Hasn't his band been wiped out?"

Zha Geli shook his head, "Brother Long and a few of his

fellow bandits escaped. We must try to lure the Wo Guli's band of bandits out the Mengna Forest and eliminate them. We must avoid letting any of them slip from our hands!"

At that moment, Qiao La had left the Chinese honey locust tree and, arching his back, sneaked into the bushes.

Guo Long became anxious, "Oh no! He's getting the rifles. He's got a horse in the forest!"

Zha Geli said, "If this batch of weapons fell into the hands of Wo Guli, it would present a great difficulty to our effort to suppress the bandits. We must overtake him to get the rifles before he can."

"I'll go. I know where the subterranean cave is. I've tied a mushroom to the branch of a bush plant. I know the path leading to it. Let me go, please!"

Guo Long spoke so quickly in a breath as if he were pouring beans from a bamboo tube.

But there was no response.

He grew more anxious. Raising his head, he caught sight of two pair of eyes gazing at him.

"Why? You don't trust me?" cried out Guo Long. "If it had not been for me, how would you have known about Qiao La?"

The response to Guo Long was still the same quiet gazes.

"I…," Guo Long was speechless.

Grandpa Du Ba heaved a deep sigh and ran his hand gently over Guo Long's red-cloth headwear.

"Child, only white-vented bulbuls know how many trees there are on Mount Beilu. I can read your Uncle Zha Geli's mind. You're eager to avenge your parents, very eager. But you're a fledgling red junglefowl after all. You've built your nest on a lonely tree, which is me. I want to see you fly and listen to you sing. But I also fear to see your wings broken by the wind and your feathers wet by the rain…"

Grandpa Du Ba could not go on for a moment. His voice became hoarse. After a pause, he turned to Zha Geli,

"Zha Geli, let him go, please! I know the child. He's up to the task! Besides, we three have to part company and be on our own anyway."

Grandpa Du Ba's words made Guo Long's feelings surge. For a time, he felt that he had a lot to say to him and to Uncle Zha Geli.

But he said only this:

"I…I won't let you down!"

Zha Geli pulled him in his arms and held him tight,

"You're a good boy, Guo Long! We've got all our hope on you! You must get ahead of Qiao La and do a clean job so that he'll come away empty-handed. Then he'll have to lie to Wo Guli and won't dare to tell the truth of losing the rifles even till he dies."

Guo Long was about to set off when Zha Geli pulled him by the arm,

"Let me ask you. What will you do when you get the rifles?"

"Well…,' Guo Long scratched his head.

Well, I was only thinking of getting the rifles. What am I

going to do with them afterward?

Grandpa Du Ba said, "Guo Long, what do we do when we hunt down a big animal but can't take it back?"

Grandpa Du Ba's elicitation reminded Guo Long. Patting his forehead, he said,

"I got it! I'll bring a spade with me. When I get the rifles, I'll dig a pit and hide them in it. A good idea?"

"Good! Zha Geli nodded, "You see, no matter how anxious we may be, if we calm down to think hard, we'll have good ideas! Well, hurry and go! Return to the tavern as soon as you finish!"

"You may rest assured!"

After he finished, Guo Long dashed into the hardy banana grove. He took a small spade from the tavern and went into the dense forest.

Grandpa Du Ba did not withdraw his eyes until Guo Long disappeared in the distance.

"Zha Geli, it's time I've got to dash!"

What? Zha Geli felt his heart skip a beat. Grandpa Du Ba did read my mind!

"Zha Geli, don't worry about my physical condition. I'll get to Galuo Village before the sun touches the mountaintop. Tell me if you've got something else for me to do!"

Zha Geli felt Grandpa Du Ba's words heart-warming.

Great minds think alike!

Grandpa Du Ba knew every plan that Zha Geli had on his mind.

"Grandpa," Zha Geli's voice quivered a bit, "There's a mole in Galuo Village working for the bandits. We don't know who he is yet. So, never let anyone know about the plan to lure the bandits out of the forest. Go directly to Company Commander Qi, and tell him about our plan only. Never ever let the word out!"

"No, never." Grandpa Du Ba nodded, "Zha Geli, each of us three is now on his own, but you've got the heaviest responsibility! I know you must catch up with Qiao La, shadow him, and make sure he can deliver the charcoal to Wo Guli's hands without any trouble. For Wo Guli to get this piece of charcoal is key to our plan's success!" Grandpa Du Ba paused a little and continued, "To carry this plan through, you've got to follow him to the lair of the bandits, the lair of man-eating tigers!"

Zha Geli said, "Grandpa, don't you often refer to me as a tiger of the Aini people? How can a tiger be scared of tigers?"

Grandpa Du Ba sighed, still gazing into Zha Geli's eyes, "The Aini people have such as saying: 'A tiger opens one of its eyes even in sleep.' So, you must be careful…!" After a pause, Grandpa Du Ba glanced at Mount Beilu and continued,

"Don't forget your wife is still waiting for you to come home!"

Perhaps Grandpa Du Ba should not have introduced the topic at a moment like this.

But he did.

He said what he said at such a moment.

A gust of wind sprang up and rustled the lush leaves of the trees.

A word threw Zha Geli's heart into turmoil.

Don't forget.

How can I?

Suddenly, a pair of beautifully teary eyes appeared before Zha Geli's mind's eye...

His wife Na Sha watched Zha Geli packing without saying a word. He was ready to set off, but she was still sitting on the shakedown holding her knees with her hands. She had been gazing quietly at her husband with her beautiful eyes sparkling in the light of the fire pit.

"I've got to go, Na Sha!" said Zha Geli softly.

There was no response.

Na Sha's eyes were glistening.

They were filled with tears like twin lakes.

Zha Geli went up to her and held her cheeks in his hands.

"I'll be back when I complete my task. Look at you! Are you okay?"

"I'm fine!" Na Sha turned her face aside to shy away from Zha Geli's eyes, "I've a hunch that this time, things won't be so simple..."

His wife foresaw something ominous!

For a time, Zha Geli was speechless. He looked up at his son Little Lige, who was fast asleep.

Little Lige was only four years old. He broke into a smile

in his sleep.

A drop of saliva trickled from the corner of his mouth down his chubby cheek.

What's he dreaming of?

Zha Geli had promised to get him the most beautiful fire-tailed sunbird. But he was too busy to do so. Blinking his eyes, Little Lige asked Zha Geli before going to bed last night,

"Ada, when are you going to get me a bird?"

"Tomorrow" was Zha Geli's response.

"Tomorrow, tomorrow, but when is tomorrow?"

Little Lige threw himself into Zha Geli's arms and rubbed the stubble of his ada's chin with his hand.

"Tomorrow is…" Pointing at the dark of the night outside the stilt bamboo house, Zha Geli said, "Well, tomorrow is when my sweetheart Little Lige has had a good sleep and opened his eyes to see the day break. That will be tomorrow…"

"Will you get me a bird when day breaks again?"

"Yes, I will."

Now, Little Lige had hope.

He lay down with satisfaction.

He had just closed his eyes when he opened them again:

"Ada, I want a fire-tailed sunbird!"

"Okay, I'll get you a fire-tailed sunbird!"

With complete satisfaction, Little Lige closed his eyes.

Before long, he fell asleep.

He went to sleep, hoping that it would be daybreak when he woke up.

Smiling in his sleep, he must have dreamt of the fire-tailed sunbird.

Yes, when I'm back this time, I'll get him a fire-tailed sunbird no matter what!

As he was thinking so, Zha Geli bent over and ran his hand over his sleeping son's forehead covered in beads of sweat.

He had veined, coarse hands that were very strong. But when he put one on his son's forehead, it was so gentle and soft, lest he might startle him from his dream.

With his hand on his son's forehead, he remembered what Company Commander Qi had told him,

"Zha Geli, I've got a son, too. He's as old as Little Lige and also has a chubby face. I haven't seen him for two or three years. He's with his mom in our hometown Hebei…"

Hebei? Zha Geli did not know where it was, but it must have been a far, faraway place.

Why did Company Commander Qi have to leave his wife and son behind and come all the way to the border area over mountains and across rivers?

He came so that the children in the border area can smile in their dreams and that mothers here don't have to weep in secret.

With the thinking, he stepped out of his house, left his wife and son, and hurried into the vast morning fog…

Why do people have to have feelings?

And why are feelings so tormenting...?

Now, Grandpa Du Ba's words threw Zha Geli's heart into turmoil again.

His wife's teary eyes and his son's smiling face appeared before his mind's eye at once.

Zha Geli felt a feeling beyond description surging in his heart...

Is there a feeling more affectionate than the one between husband and wife in this world?

Is there a feeling more loving than the one between father and son in this world?

Who can answer these questions?

For a time, Grandpa Du Ba and Zha Geli both fell silent.

Their big hands held each other tight.

They parted company without further ado.

They parted company so that wives would not have to be separated from their husbands!

They parted company so that sons would not have to be separated from their fathers!

They parted company so that grandsons would not have to be separated from their grandfathers!

Grandpa Du Ba, with his back slightly hunched, disappeared on the mountain path leading to Mount Beilu.

Zha Geli walked vigorously and briskly. He eventually caught up with Qiao La and shadowed him unnoticed.

Chapter 7

Qiao La trekked a long time in the thick forest. He finally found the horse he had tethered to the tropical almond tree.

He felt lucky that everything had gone smoothly so far.

Leading the horse, he resumed his tread into the depth of the old-growth forest.

Zha Geli pussyfooted behind him, neither too far nor too close, using the trees for cover.

The further he followed Qiao La, the more anxious he became:

Has Guo Long found the rifles?

Has he removed the rifles from the cave?

Did he have enough time to get the rifles and then hide them?

……

Qiao La finally reached the Malayan yellowwood.

He glanced sideways to make sure that there was no one around. Then he stopped the horse, stooped down, and reached to lift the board cover off the cave opening.

Now the moment of truth!

Zha Geli's heart almost stopped beating.

What if Ge Long failed to anticipate Qiao La so that the latter was able to get the rifles and ammo?

Getting them back from Qiao La is out of the question. That would startle him, and he's expected to deliver the charcoal to Wo Guli.

Neither is inaction an option: How can I see him shipping the rifles and ammo back to his bandit lair?

It's really a hard decision!

Qiao La could never imagine that behind him there would be a man whose heart was afire with anxiety.

"Hi-yah!" Summing up all his strength, Qiao La lifted the thick board cover.

Suddenly, he plopped to the ground as if he were bitten by a snake!

The cave was empty. There was not even a stick in it!

Zha Geli heaved a silent sigh of relief behind the tree…

Good job, Guo Long!

Chapter 8

Guo Long was very efficient at getting and hiding the rifles.

After he finished, he picked a narrow, winding trail leading to the tavern, his small spade in hand.

As he treaded through the dense forest, he had to pull apart the vines blocking his way.

He trekked and trekked when, all of a sudden, there sprang out a tiger from behind the trees!

This was a Bengal tiger with a stature as large as that of a bull. It had a reddish orange coat of short and glossy hair. Highlighting its body were vertical brown stripes that formed into a few diamond shapes on both sides of its belly. It was dragging its stiff but not too thick tail across the grass. The stripe pattern on its forehead resembled the Chinese character 王, meaning "king." Under it, a pair of walnut-sized eyes shone with a greenish glow. Its mouth opened slightly, baring two knife-sharp fangs.

Guo Long was dumbfounded. A shudder ran through him from head to toe like lightning. He fixed his eyes on the tiger's hairy face.

The long and dense hairs all over its face betrayed the tiger's old age.

Guo Long had learned from Grandpa Du Ba that the tigers in the Mengna Forest feared people by nature so that they would not launch preempt attacks against them.

They would not unless they were provoked.

Nevertheless, two kinds of tigers are exceptions.

One is the injured.

The other is the aged.

Injured or aged, they are slow in action. Having lost their previous stamina and prowess, they can no longer catch animals that can run on their nimble hoofed legs. Therefore, they often go hungry. They are often so starved that they cannot even roar. Their stomach growling for food, they are apt to attack people. Experience tells these tigers that people are easier to overwhelm than animals and that they do not have to chase or battle them: They feel weak at the mere sight of a tiger. A gentle wipe with the front paw can easily sweep a person to the ground.

Eating people has become these tigers' lifestyle.

Blocking Guo Long's way was such a man-eating tiger!

This was the second time that Guo Long had run into a man-eating tiger.

The first time happened in the morning of a late autumn three years ago.

That morning, Guo Long was collecting mushrooms in the forest when suddenly a tiger dashed out of a thicket. Apparently, it had lost a battle to a bull not long before since its recently scabbed nose and mouth were still covered in blood stains. One of its front paws seemed to be injured as it wobbled when walking. Gnawing hunger forced it to attempt at people as its food. Bare-handed, Guo Long did not dare to run because running would spur the tiger to pursue and catch up with him. But how could he deal with it without running away? He was at a loss. Seeing Guo Long motionless, the tiger growled and inched forward. Since it was the first time it tried to attack a person, its man-fearing instinct deterred it from pouncing upon Guo Long. It was lucky of the desperate Guo Long that he suddenly spotted a midsized tree by him. It was an antiaris toxicaria tree, nicknamed "death upon touch" for its extremely poisonous sap. He gingerly broke a branch off and pointed its white sap-oozing tip at the tiger. The beast seemed to recognize the potency of the poison; for it faltered and balked. Taking the opportunity, Guo Long climbed swiftly up another tree nearby. Tigers are not tree climbers. While he had been taking refuge on the tree, the tiger had waited under it. After almost a day's stalemate, the tiger had left in a huff.

Now Guo Long ran into another man-eating tiger.

Guo Long looked around, hoping to find a "death upon touch" tree again.

But how could they be so easy to come by?

According to Grandpa Du Ba, there were only about ten "death upon touch" trees in the entire Mengna Forest.

What shall I do?

He had only the little spade in his hands!

This man-eating tiger glared at him with a nasty look, exhaling a breath of fishiness from its mouth. It dug its claws extending from their sheaths into the ground and licked its tough whiskers with its tongue covered in sharp, rear-facing projections.

How ferocious it was!

When young, it might have smacked many a muntjac's or red deer's head with its strong front paws and broken many a dhole's or wild boar's neck with it sharp fangs.

Now that it was old, it was going to eat people.

It had long lost its natural man-fearing instinct; what was left of it was only its cold-heartedness.

Guo Long was fully aware that the man-eating tiger could pounce upon him at any moment. *How can I fight it with only a spade?*

He was being terror-stricken when suddenly Grandpa Du Ba's words rang in his ear:

"If a tiger lunges toward you, make a sudden move, and it will scare it. It will then be stupefied and at a loss what to do."

Grandpa's words emboldened Guo Long. He suddenly let out a roar.

"Roarrrr!"

Meanwhile, "whoosh!" he flung the small space at the tiger's face.

Sure enough, the tiger was briefly stupefied. Tilting its neck aside, it dodged the spade. Then it also roared, so loud that it shook the leaves rustling off trees.

Before the sound of its roar died down, it arched its back and "swiz!" pounced upon Guo Long.

But it unexpectedly missed its target.

Guo Long had climbed up a tree like a monkey.

The wrathful tiger threw itself upon the tree, stood up, and reached out its front paws trying to seize Guo Long's feet.

It was a close call: The tiger was only a paw's way from Guo Long.

The steaming breath from the tiger's mouth gave his feet a sensation.

If he had been a bit slower, the tiger would have pulled him down the tree. Even a strike of its paw would end his life.

There are pieces of meat and flesh caught between the claws, but a tiger cannot lick them clean. The remnants started to decay in due time and became poisonous. A scratch could be lethal to its victim.

Having missed Guo Long, the tiger flew into a rage and began to scratch the tree at random.

Screeching! Screeching!

Large pieces of the bark were scratched off, revealing the milky sapwood of the trunk.

However, unwilling to give up, it kept scratching. Then it alternated scratching with gnawing.

Wiping the sweat off his face, Guo Long took a glance at the tiger below.

Exhausted, the tiger had flopped to the ground to take a break. It occasionally raised its head to glare at Guo Long on the tree.

After they were glaring at each other for a while, Guo Long resumed climbing. The tiger also recuperated and went on scratching the tree.

It wanted to scratch the tree down so that Guo Long would fall to the ground.

Guo Long was by no means out of danger.

He was climbing further up when suddenly his head bumped into something neither soft nor hard.

He looked up and was taken aback!

It was a bloody leg!

Ah! Where did this bloody leg come from?

Taking a closer look through the thick foliage, he saw a red deer placed over a bough. Half of its body had been eaten.

Having been venturing in the old-growth forest with Grandpa Du Ba over the years, Guo Long knew immediately that this was the work of an adult leopard.

Leopards are nimble, cunning climbers. They can climb up a tree no matter how tall it is. A leopard often dashes up to a tree to catch a monkey. It frequently lies on a big bough silently in wait for a prey passing by under the tree. Not big in stature, it can attack an animal two or three times its size. If it cannot finish eating a prey for one meal, it will hide the remaining part by hanging it high on a tree and returns to it when hungry.

Guo Long was excited at the sight of the remaining half of the red deer's carcass.

He carefully caught a crotch of the tree to steady himself. He then freed both his hands and pulled the mangled red deer carcass over and pushed it down with great effort. It thudded onto the ground.

The startled tiger dodged it.

After a while, the tiger found he remaining half of a red deer. It presented itself as a windfall. The beast roared with jubilance.

It was about to enjoy the red deer when suddenly there leapt out a leopard from the bushes.

Without further ado, the leopard lunged over, grabbed the red deer in its mouth, and dashed into the depth of the forest.

As it happened, the owner of the carcass had returned to claim it.

Normally, fierce as it is, a leopard never fights with a tiger.

It was a different story this time. For one thing, the leopard would not bear the tiger to seize its own food. For another, it knew that the tiger was old and easy to deal with. That was why it came back pouncing on the carcass and retrieved what it claimed to be its own.

The tiger was enraged by the leopard that deprived it of its delicious meal.

It would not take it lying down albeit its old age.

A tiger is a tiger. After all, it is the king of the animal world, as was proclaimed by the royal-insignia-like stripe pattern on its forehead.

With a roar, it sprang to run after the leopard.

As the leopard scampered, the tiger was hot on its trail, leaving behind the broken branches of trees and bushes rustling behind it. The two natural enemies darted into the depth of the forest one after another.

Now the opportunity came. Guo Long climbed down the tree, recollected himself, and rushed in the direction toward the exit of the forest.

After running a few steps, he suddenly stopped. *No, I can't run against the wind, which will send my body odor back.*

In case the tiger fails to catch up with the leopard, it'll turn around to look for me.

Man-eating tigers are the most sensitive to odors.

So, I must follow the wind.

As he made his decision, Guo Long turned around and ran before the wind.

He ran and ran, with the sole purpose of fleeing the tiger. But he did not realize that he had lost his bearings until he felt fatigued.

He found nothing but trees in dim light around him, as if he had entered into a huge sac.

Occasionally, he saw a few bluish will-o'-the-wisps flickering deep in the forest.

A red-haired passer-by guest had told Guo Long that the will-o'-the-wisps were the flames of the fire lit by the ghosts of men who had died from injustice. They used the bluish flames to barbecue meat. If someone treated them badly, they would run after him and burned him to ashes with the bluish flames. If he treated them well, they would shine the way for him so that he could find his way.

Later, Grandpa Du Ba told Long Guo that these flames were not lit by ghosts. They were the light of phospho-rescence caused by gases from decaying plants or animal carcasses.

Now, Guo Long saw the will-o'-the-wisps again. And they were everywhere.

Where am I?

Where's the tavern?

Guo Long wiped the sweat off his face and looked around.

It was quiet all around.

Will-o'-the-wisps were flickering here and there.

Guo Long recalled what the red-haired passer-by guest had told him?

Are the flickering will-o'-the-wisps really the flames lit by ghosts of people who died of injustice?

Are they shining the way for me?

If so, then among them, there must be the flames lit by my ada and ama.

Which cluster of the will-o'-the-wisps were ignited by them?

How did they know that their beloved son Guo Long is here?

Ada, ama! You died so miserably!

Are those flames along with yours lit by the villagers also murdered by the bandits?

You all died of injustice. But the days of the murderous bandits are numbered!

Guo Long was gazing transfixed at the will-o'-the-wisps when suddenly an inexplicable danger loomed behind and gave him a shudder.

A man was behind him!

A man with an average stature!

The heat of his breath assailed the back of Guo Long's neck.

Before Guo Long turned around, wham! a wooden club struck him on the head.

Guo Long blacked out and lost consciousness...

Chapter 9

When Guo Long opened his eyes, he found himself lying in a promiscuous heap of grass, with his head covered in a big vine leaf.

Am I dreaming?

He blinked his eyes hard, only to see clearly that he was lying in a shack built of tree branches and twigs.

The shack was covered watertight with vines and big, lush leaves.

Two men, one tall and the other short, were sitting around a fire pit murmuring.

The taller man had brawny limbs, thick brows, and bulging eyes. His thick, shriveled hair escaped from his black-cloth headwear and covered his ears.

He was sitting opposite Guo Long. While looking down at the fire that he was stoking, he did not notice that Guo Long had gained consciousness.

The short man sat on a thick tree trunk about a meter in height facing the other way from Guo Long. He was smoking gurgling a bamboo water pipe. Light in the shack was dim, so that the flickering tobacco glow outline the smoker's silhouette from time to time: He was thin and small as well as a bit hunchbacked. He wore only one silver earring, which glittered conspicuously.

However, Guo Long could not discern the features of the man wearing the single earring. From his stature, Guo Long could tell that he was the one that had struck him and knocked him out.

What are these two men doing?

Why are they in the old-growth forest teeming with beasts of prey?

Just then, the taller man raised his head.

Guo Long closed his eyes just in time.

He heard him talking in a low, muffled voice,

"We haven't had salt in our food for days. I can't even move my arms and legs. When we storm out of the forest and launch our attack, I'll get nothing but a sack of salt so I can enjoy a few days of tasty meals!"

What? Storming out and launching an attack?

The shorter man nodded,

"You're right! But we aren't sure if our chief Wo Guli

has made up his mind or not!"

What?

Wo Guli!

Guo Long felt his heart skipping a beat.

It's terrible! I'm now in the hands of Wo Guli's bandits.

I've just fled the tiger's lair only to end up in the wolves' den.

What shall I do?

Holding his breath, he moved his hands gently. He felt his hands free of bondage.

He then wiggled his feet, and they were free as well.

With both my hands and feet free, I'll pretend to be senseless. I'll keep my eyes closed and wait for my opportunity.

Guo Long shut his eyes tight. But pricking his ears, he listened carefully.

After a while, Guo Long figured out something from their conversation…

The taller man was named Zhuang Tie.

The shorter one was called Duo Piao.

The two thugs were talking about whether Wo Guli had decided to attack Galuo Village tomorrow morning or not.

Then, they shifted their topic to Guo Long.

Duo Piao mumbled, "Well? Why hasn't this rascal woken up?"

"I think we don't have to wait for him to wake up," said Zhuang Tie in his low, muffled voice, "Let's open another mouth in his forehead!"

Ah! They're going to kill me, and that's for real! I'll leap up and fight them till the end!

I'll die anyway. If I can leave some scratch and bite marks on them, I won't die in vain!

Guo Long was ready for a fight.

Gurgling, gurgling! While smoking his bamboo water pipe, Duo Piao broke into a sinister laugh,

"If I wanted to kill him, why did I just gave him a couple of strikes?"

"But what's the use of keeping him alive?"

Gurgling, gurgling!

Duo Piao puffed unhurriedly.

"You tell me! Why did a teenager like him come here to risk so many beasts of prey? Did he lose his bearings? Or is he up to something? We don't know his intent yet, so why can't we get some answers from him?"

"Hey, you're as smart as a fox!"

With what he had overheard from their conversation, Guo Long started contemplating.

The two thugs don't know my intent!

They're going to get some answers from me when I wake up!

They don't know my intent, but I know theirs now.

Their current concern is whether their fellow bandits are going to attack Galuo Village tomorrow. Only I know the answer.

Guo Long became excited. He rolled over.

Immediately afterward, he mumbled half distinctly,

"…Wo, Wo…Gu…li…"

The trick worked wonders.

The two men by the fire pit immediately raised their heads startled. They fixed their eyes on Guo Long's face at the same time.

"Woke up?" murmured Duo Piao to himself.

"Yes, he woke up," Zhuang Tie responded foolishly.

"What did he say?" Duo Piao went on murmuring to himself.

Zhuang Tie echoed, "I didn't quite catch what he said."

"Well?" Duo Piao tilted his head and pricked his ears.

Zhuang Tie also did the same stupidly, "Well?"

Guo Long held back his laughter and lowered his voice as much as possible,

"…Wo, Chief Wo Guli…someone hit…hit me…"

This time, Duo Piao and Zhuang Tie heard him clearly.

They sprang up like shrimps in a hot pan. Together, they threw themselves to Guo Long.

Grasping Guo Long by the collar, Duo Piao shook him repeatedly, "Wake up! Wake up! Wake up!"

The big earring kept swaying from his ear.

Guo Long was still mumbling semi-consciously,

"…water…water…"

"Go and get some water!" yelled Duo Piao.

Zhuang Tie hastily handed him a bamboo tube of water.

Duo Piao helped Guo Long sit up and placed the tube to

his mouth.

While sipping the water, Guo Long went on mumbling:

"...Wo Guli... Chief..."

After a while, Guo Long felt that he had faked enough unconsciousness to be convincing and opened his eyes.

"Who are you...?"

Duo Piao grinned, "He-he-he! We're...we're... Well, you're home!"

"Home? Who're you guys? Who hit me?"

Duo Piao shook his head and the single earring simultaneously, "No one hit you! You were so tired from running that you bumped into a tree and passed out. We saved your life!"

"Really?" Suppressing his anger, Guo Long feigned a smile, "Thank you for doing so!"

Duo Piao asked, "Why are you here in the old forest?"

"I..." shying away from Duo Piao's suspicious eyes, Guo Long stuttered, "I...I came to collect mushrooms but got lost."

Zhuang Tie could not help asking, "Hey, don't hem and haw with us! Didn't you mumble about Chief Wo Guli?"

Guo Long pretended to be alarmed.

Duo Piao shot a glare at Zhuang Tie and turned to Guo Long with a beam, "Child, don't be scared. Tell us what you know. Are you looking for Wo Guli?"

Guo Long asked back, "You know him?"

Zhuang Tie was impatient again, "Hey, what do you mean by knowing him? We're all his men."

Shooting another glare at Zhuang Tie, Duo Piao admonished silently, "You big mouth! Are we trying to get some answers from him or you?" But since Zhuang Tie had already revealed their identity, Duo Piao had to follow up with the thread of conversation.

"Yes, we're both Wo Guli's men. If you've got something to let us know, just spill it out!"

Blinking his eyes, Guo Long said, "Someone asked me to deliver an urgent message to him. Take me to him in a hurry!"

Duo Piao asked in a haste, "Where's the message?"

Guo Long opened his mouth wide.

What? In your mouth? The two bandits were dumbfounded.

The quicker-thinking Duo Piao blurted out,

"You mean it's an oral message, don't you? What's so urgent? Tell us first."

Guo Long shook his head and responded, "If you're really Wo Guli's men, you should take me to him as soon as possible. Only I can pass the oral message to him."

Duo Piao's cunning eyes licked Guo Long's face up and down like the tongue of a cow. With knitted brows, he remained quiet for a long while.

Guo Long knew that they were only a little convinced.

Feigning honesty, Guo Long sighed, "As a matter of fact, it's nothing confidential. It's about whether we're going to attack Galuo Village tomorrow morning."

"What?" Duo Piao and Zhuang Tie exclaimed in chorus.

Guo Long's bombshell made the two bandits almost completely credulous.

"Are we going to attack it after all?" Zhuang Tie was anxious.

Duo Piao also gazed into Guo Long's eyes.

Guo Long said, "If one of you can lead me to the chief, then you will both know." Pausing a little, he continued, "Originally, I didn't have to deliver the oral message. It was a message that should have been picked up by someone called…called Qiao La. But we waited and waited, but he didn't show up. So, I was asked to deliver it in person."

"Really?" responded Duo Piao and Zhuang Tie in chorus.

The two men had but to trust Guo Long because what he told them was so specific that he even mentioned Qiao La's name.

"Alright!" Duo Piao rose, picked up his tailing-pointed knife and tucked it in his waist, "Let's go! I'll take you to the chief!"

Zhuang Tie said, "Let me take him there!"

Duo Piao said, "You wait here, and we'll let you know the result!"

"Okay," responded Zhuang Tie. "Only if we can beat the drum early!"

What? Drum?

Guo Long intuitively glanced over the shack.

Only then did he discover that Duo Piao was sitting on a drum instead of a tree trunk.

A wooden drum!

A wooden drum is a section of a tree trunk, but it is hollowed and has a row of holes chiseled through the middle of the shaft. It is like the wooden-fish bell used by a Mahayana Buddhist priest during religious rituals. The drum sounds deafening when beaten with a wooden drumstick.

It is imaginable that the sound of "Boom-bah-bah-boom! Boom-bah-bah-boom!" can reach far and wide in such a quiet forest.

Having a clear view of the drum, Guo Long questioned himself:

What's the wooden drum used for?

What did he mean when Zhuang Tie said he expected to beat the drum early?

But he could not answer them.

Duo Piao demanded, "Let's go!"

Guo Long set out with him.

He was by no means going to see Wo Guli.

It was unnecessary!

Nor could he go!

He wanted to get out of this wolves' den by winning the bandits' trust.

He thought that there must be a chance to flee on the way to Wo Guli's lair.

Guo Long overestimated the possibility of an escape.

Duo Piao followed him closely all the way, never letting his eyes stray from him.

They had trekked a long time before Guo Long could find any opportunity.

He broke into sweat on his forehead.

Finally, Duo Piao spoke:

"We're almost there!"

This announcement sounded like a rock crashing upon Guo Long's head.

His heart sank and his brain nearly went blank.

A step further was a step closer to Wo Guli.

If he really stood in front of Wo Guli and be asked for the oral message, then his identity would be exposed.

No, I can't go to see Wo Guli.

Seeing him means the end of my life.

I have no other alternative than fight to the bitter end with Duo Piao!

But how? He's not easy to mess with.

Besides, I'm barehanded, while he has a knife. If I start a fight, I'm certainly no match for him.

No! He must die! Not me!

Guo Long was racking his brain when he suddenly spotted a snake.

It was a tiger keelback (rhabdophis tigrinus) viper!

A victim, once bitten, cannot walk ten steps away before dropping dead.

Guo Long walked a couple of steps, turned around abruptly, and cried out in alarm:

"A viper!"

Duo Piao, who was now behind Guo Long, was taken aback and turned around involuntarily, thus pointing his buttocks to Guo Long.

Guo Long scooped up the tiger keelback swiftly and, holding it like a spear, thrusted it in Duo Piao's buttocks.

When Duo Piao realized what had happened, the viper had punctured his pants with its venomous fangs.

"Ouch!"

Duo Piao let out a bloodcurdling scream and widened his bulging eyes. He reached his hand out to grab the tiger keelback snake, his big earring swaying with his every move.

Guo Long let go the snake and took flight. Suddenly, he felt a tinge of warmth on his wrist.

The tiger keelback, now in Duo Biao's hand, had bitten Guo Long as well.

It was a serious bite. Pain surged from the wrist to his heart instantly.

Guo Long staggered forward while sucking blood and poison from his wrist and spitting them out.

"See if you can get away from me! Where're you running? Where're you running?"

Widening his bloodshot eyes and holding the snake in both hands, Duo Piao was hot in pursuit, his earring swaying as he ran.

Guo Long's act of sucking the venom out of his wrist reminded Duo Piao: If he could not get it out of his body, he would hardly survive. Unfortunately, he could do nothing.

The snake bite was on his butt, so how could he suck the poison out?

The flame of poison was burning toward his heart. Duo Piao felt that all the blood in his body was about to squirt out.

His call gradually weakened, and his legs began to get out of control.

His angry expression was slowly freezing.

As a matter of fact, he could have been able to grab Guo Long by reaching out his arm.

But he found it hard to shorten the distance.

Guo Long ran and ran until he could hear no footsteps behind him.

Looking back, Duo Piao had been covered with blood!

Purplish blood oozing from his mouth had dyed his whole body.

The viper had struggled out of Duo Piao's grip and wriggled its body to wind around his neck three or four times. As it coiled, the snake squeezed its body tighter and tighter until...

Thump!

Like a tree felled down, the bloody Duo Piao threw himself to the ground on his face.

Holding out a convulsive hand, he screamed with the little strength left of him:

"See if you can get away…!"

Guo Long stood stupefied for a second before running again.

But he had just run a few steps when he felt his whole body burning.

Thump!

He collapsed as well…

Chapter 10

Guo Long did not die. He had just passed out.

The tiger keelback viper had bitten Duo Piao first and injected most of its venom into him. When it bit Guo Long, it did not have much of the venom left.

Besides, Guo Long had sucked them out and thereby survived the venomous attack.

After no one knows how long, he could feel his face hurt and itchy.

He opened his eyes, only to see himself besieged by a swarm of big red ants.

Taking him as a corpse, the ants crawled all over him even into his nostrils. More kept coming as reinforcement. If all the thousands of ants should start gnawing at him at once, he would eventually become a skeleton.

Guo Long quickly sprang up on his feet and patted the ants off him.

His bitten face was swollen and looked as bumpy as an old corn ear without its husks.

As he patted off the ants with his right hand, he felt that he could not lift his left hand.

He took a look only to find his snake-bitten wrist swollen like a small tree trunk.

A gust of wind came smelling fishy.

Duo Piao lay upon his face, and his contorted limps and body were telling the misery that he had suffered before his death.

Guo Long pulled out his tailing-pointed knife from his waist, scooped some of the fallen leaves with it, and covered the body.

Now, he began to feel throbbing pain in his arm. The snake venom was trying to destroy it.

While enduring the pain, Guo Long was searching the old-growth forest for devil pepper (rauvolfia verticillata), an herb that could be used as a snake venom antidote.

This is a plant with an opposite leaf arrangement. After chewed and plastered on the wound, it can kill pain, reduce swelling, and detoxify snake venom.

Guo Long remembered an adage favored by Grandpa Du Ba: A'ao'abo, god of everything in the universe, created rodents as well as cats.

As he milled in the old-growth forest, Guo Long murmured a prayer silently:

"I pray to you, A'ao'abo! Please give me some devil pepper! Please give me some devil pepper!"

Suddenly, his eyes lit up! There was a devil pepper plant in a thick growth of grass not far away.

Has A'ao'abo answered my prayer?

Guo Long rushed over, pulled the devil pepper plant out, shook the dirt off, and placed its bitter root in his mouth to chew.

Just then, he heard human voices.

Ah, is A'ao'abo talking to me?

Guo Long was astonished!

He could not believe his ears. He tilted his head aside and, cupping his hand over his ear, listened intensely.

There was no mistake. He heard people talking in the forest indeed.

Guo Long sneaked toward the source of the voices under the cover of the trees.

Who are talking here?

The closer Guo Long inched, the faster his heart thumped.

Finally, he saw a shed hidden in the thickets and vines.

This was a big shed constructed of tree branches, which were so thick that roots and leaves could grow from them when planted in the ground.

At this moment, there were two people under a big tree outside the shed, one standing and the other sitting.

Sitting on a tree stump was a plump old man with a square face, on which a pair of round eyes gleamed like those of a hawk. He wore a bristling beard as tough as iron wire. He had a large mouth of thick, everted lips of a purplish red color, which made him look avaricious. Sitting on the stump, he was trimming his beard with a dagger.

The glittering blade drew lightning streaks back and forth over his gloomy, swar-thy face.

"…son of a gun! He dared to undermine his own people. He's more deadly than our enemy!"

As he was trimming his beard, the plump old man scolded.

Who's he scolding?

"How dare he double-cross me Wo Guli, stealing my deal like bearding the lion in its den!"

What? Wo Guli?

Can this plump old man be Wo Guli?

Widening his eyes, Guo Long sized up this devil that he had slaughtered many times in his dream.

Snipping, snipping, snipping! Wo Guli was still trimming his beard.

He killed people the same way he snipped his beard.

And the people he had slaughtered way outnumber the hairs of his beard he was removing.

But he did not appear brutal whatsoever.

He might look amiable if he smiled.

But he did not smile.

"Darn! He pushed us over thinking we sent too few people!"

Then, the man who sat with his back to Guo Long spoke,

"It's true. Brother Long has no consideration for our feelings!"

Guo Long recognized this familiar voice.

When he looked closely, sure enough, it was Qiao La!

He overheard Qiao La saying, "If he thinks he's capable, then he should've fought the Red Han.[3] We're not suppressing them anyway! …Zhe Mu and I had just gotten hold of the rifles when Bother Long's people besieged us and grabbed the rifles without giving a reason. Zhe Mu was so angry that he fought back and was thus chopped to death. They didn't kill me because they wanted me to bring a message to you, saying that they were just borrowing the rifles and ammo…"

Now Guo Long understood what they were talking about.

Just as Zha Geli had expected, Qiao La concealed the fact that he had lost the rifles. He fabricated a story to tell Wo Guli and shifted the blame onto Brother Long instead.

In fact, when Qiao La fought with Mang Ga, none of them said anything. That is to say, they were not acquainted with each other. Then, why was Qiao Lao so sure that he was from Brother Long's band?

Obviously, the double-headed snake tattoo on his chest gave him the hint.

---

[3] Red Han, is a pejorative term that the bandits used to refer to the PLA force because it consisted mostly of ethnic Han commanders and fighters dispatched to the border area inhabited mostly by minority ethnic peoples.

Zha Geli's judgment was correct: The tattoo was the symbol of the bandits led by Brother Long.

Just then, there came out a small, thin man from the shed. He had thin brows, narrow eyes, and thin lips.

After he was out of the shed, he raised his head, eyed Wo Guli and Qiao La, and said in a high pitch with a wave of his hand,

"Forget it! Forget it! When a tiger and a leopard are locked in a fight, mind you, the Himalayan blue sheep that they're fighting for may escape. I may not have seen Brother Long, but I know he's battling with the Red Han. It's better for the rifles to fall into his hands than to those of the army-civilian joint defense team, isn't it?"

Both Wo Guli and Qiao La was speechless.

One was suppressing his anger.

The other found a way out.

After a long while, Wo Guli opened his palm and fixed his eyes on it, with a somber countenance. He gazed at his hand for quite some time before he looked up and glanced at the small thin man.

"Wind will arise in the old-growth forest when it threatens rain. The setback Qiao La and Zhe Mu suffered today is a bad omen. If we go out of the forest and attack Galuo Village tomorrow…"

He just stopped short.

Wo Guli looked down again, focusing his eyes on his palm.

He had something in his palm.

What's it?

Guo Long assumed that the thing Wo Guli was holding in his hand was most likely a piece of charcoal.

Sure enough, it was verified by Qiao La...

"Chief," Qiao La was a bit impatient, "you mean we're not going to launch the attack? What I picked up is obviously a piece of charcoal!"

"Not to attack?" Wo Guli began with a rhetoric question, "Not to attack means we're waiting to be killed. If the Red Han established a foothold in the Galuo and Mengda villages, they would be as good as two crags blocking the pass of Mount Beilu. Then, we'd never be able to go out of the forest. We storm out before their main force arrives, burn the Galuo and Mengda villages down, and reduce them to ashes. Then, they'll have no joint defense teams at all! We must go out and attack them, and tomorrow is a good chance. But..." He stopped short again. With a grave look, he raked his eyes over the two men in front of him, "What we've got for the message is charcoal alright, but once out of the forest, we'll have no way to return..."

Qiao La asked, "What shall we do then?"

Wo Guli did not respond. He directed his cold eyes to the small thin man.

"Pi Luo, what do you think we should do?"

I see, this thin-browed man is named Pi Luo.

Pi Luo licked his thin lips and tilted the corner of a thin

brow, and said, "You can't get coconuts if you don't climb a coconut tree high enough. Chief, in order for us to act safely, I'll go there again to find out."

"To Galuo Village?" asked Wo Guli.

Pi Luo nodded, "Yes. I'll go to my old friend to verify it!"

"Great. Great minds think alike!" said Wo Guli, who balled his hand with the charcoal tight and crushed it. "Only you know your old friend! Go immediately. When you locate your old friend in Galuo Village, you must get solid, waterproof information from him. I'll position our men at the edge of the forest before dawn and wait for your signal. Eh…" Wo Guli paused.

He then continued, "If things remain status quo and we can get out of the forest, you fire a shot at the crows on the banyan tree. When we see the crows fly and hear them caw, we'll storm out of the forest and pounce on the villages!"

"What if things have changed?"

"If so, you set fire to the Longba Gate. When we see the fire and smoke, we'll immediately halt our offensive and withdraw into the forest."

"Okay, consider it done!"

They were as cunning as foxes!

Wo Guli was not certain as to the authenticity of the charcoal brought back by Qiao La. He wanted Pi Luo to go to his old friend to get to the bottom of it.

This "old friend" must be the bandits' mole hiding in Galuo Village!

If, by any chance, Pi Luo met this mole and learned about the arrival of the bandit-suppressing troops in the afternoon, he'd set fire to the Longba Gate.[4] *Then our plan to lure the bandits out of the forest would fall flat. The bandit-suppressing troops lying in wait on both sides of the valley would come away empty-handed.*

No!

I can't let the Longba Gate catch fire.

I must let the crows fly!

Now, the only option was to get to Galuo Village ahead of Pi Luo and report the situation to Company Commander Qi.

Guo Long's sparkling eyes searched the surroundings for a way out of the forest.

Before he found one, he suddenly heard Wo Guli saying,

"Qiao La, I know you've run an errand already, and I should've kept you here for a drink or two. But since things are urgent, I've got you other task to complete!"

Qiao La said, "Chief, just tell me what to do. I've got the legs of a red deer that knows no fatigue!"

Just then, Pi Luo came out of the shed and handed a bamboo strip to Wo Guli.

Wo Guli took it over and etched five cuts on the edge of the bamboo strip with his knife and handed it back to Qiao La.

---

[4] Longba Gate is a wooden arch at the entrance and exit of an Aini stockade village. It had human figure carvings on it. Usually, a new gate is built each year without dismantling the old one. Therefore, an Aini village usually has a long gateway. The number of the gates reveals the age of the village.

"Go to find Duo Piao. Let him beat the drum. It will give my order to rally our men to gather at the edge of the forest before dawn."

Beat the drum to give the order?

I see, the wooden drum!

Guo Long instantly recalled the wooden drum that he noticed in the shack.

Wo Guli expects his order to be issued by the drumbeat...

So, that is the function of the wooden drum!

This is terrible!

Qiao La is going to meet Duo Piao, but the latter had died already!

Once Qiao La and Zhuang Tie meet, they'll figure out everything.

Are they going to beat the drum to rally the bandits then?

Of course not!

And Qiao La would return and tell Wo Guli about the doubtable situation.

Wo Guli would surely change his mind!

Just then, he heard Qiao La saying, "Chief, I've got to dash."

Wo Guli said, "Go, and you don't have to come back. As soon as the drum sounds, you can return to your shack." As he said so, he handed a bamboo tube of wine to Qiao La and continued, "Go back and enjoy yourself. Do a good job tomorrow morning!"

Qiao La left...

…leaving Guo Long burning with anxiety.

I must catch up with Qiao La and get rid of him. I must prevent him from seeing Zhuang Tie!

But Pi Luo was also going to set off. Guo Long had to report the situation to Company Commander Qi before Pi Luo gets to the village.

Two things happened at once, but both were urgent.

Both were keys to the failure or success of the plan for the annihilation of the bandits.

However, how could Guo Long clone himself?

Now that Qiao La was about get on his way, Guo Long had no leeway for hesitation at such a critical juncture.

He made a hard choice. Pulling out his tailing-pointed knife, he trailed Qiao La.

A spark of an ambitious plan was burning into a flame in his mind…

I'll catch up with Qiao La, kill him, and goaded Zhuang Tie to beat the drum with the bamboo strip carried by Qiao La. Then I'll manage to get away from Zhuang Tie, ran at top speed out of the forest, and get to Galuo Village before dawn. And I'll tell everything I know to Company Commander Qi.

Yes, that will be what I'm going to do.

At such a crucial moment, such a bold plan striking him suddenly gave him infinite courage and strength.

Clenching his teeth and holding his knife tight, he caught up with Qiao La and shadowed him.

Chapter 11

Qiao La rushed ahead in the dense forest, start-ling wild animals out of grass from time to time.

A few foraging monkeys hopped from tree to tree above the head, knocking off some berries from it.

Shadowing Qiao La, Guo Long tried to keep himself unnoticed.

How to attack him?

While following Qiao La, Guo Long kept sizing up the situation.

Being aware that he was no match for his opponent, he had to find the best chance to get the upper hand.

For instance, when Qiao La would trip over a vine, fall into a depression in the ground, or sit down under a tree to doze off exhausted. Or, a wild animal would come out to surprise him...

However, Qiao La stepped over vines, walked around depressions, and only a squirrel jumped out of the trees...

The further he followed, the more anxious Guo Long became, and his knife-holding hand sweated profusely.

Every time Qiao La took a step forward, a step closer Guo Long approached Zhuang Tie.

I can't let him go further!

The berries falling from the trees gave Guo Long an inspiration.

He stooped down, picked up a berry, and pussyfooted rapidly closer to Qiao La.

He planned to throw the berry at Qiao La's head. When the latter stopped, he would throw himself upon Qiao La and drive the knife into his back.

He would drive the blade and the handle all the way into it.

Anxious to kill the enemy, Guo Long had only success on his mind.

Qiao La was trotting hastily.

Guo Long raised the berry.

He saw a thicket before Qiao La and held the berry above his head…

This strike would make or break!

Guo Long concentrated all his strength on his arms.

He was about to hurl the berry, when all of a sudden…

…the hurrying Qiao La stopped.

He seemed to find something odd in front of him or heard someone following him behind.

He stopped abruptly.

Guo Long was so started that he broke out in a cold sweat!

If Qiao La had turned around at this moment...

But he did not. He just stood still. He simply froze.

Now Guo Long had a reprieve.

He pussyfooted to a thick tree and hid behind it.

There, he stole a glance, only to panic at the sight!

About a dozen steps away from Qiao La, a few greyish yellow dholes were feasting upon a piece of badly mangled meat.

It looked like a deer's carcass.

No! Guo Long soon saw clearly that it was not a deer, but a man!

The dholes had torn the limbs off the mangled body.

A big earring was still hanging from one of the ears!

Ah, it was Duo Piao!

Dholes, which love to eat decomposed bodies, had dragged his body from beneath the fallen leaves.

It was this horrifying scene that had planted Qiao La's feet on the ground.

He spotted the big earring!

And he knew who the man was!

He hurriedly turned around to go back!

He was going to tell Wo Guli about it!

Qiao La's move made Guo Long worried.

But when he looked up, Qiao La was nowhere to be found!

Allowing of no more search, suddenly...

...a pair of big hands seized his neck.

Without giving a whimper, Guo Long rolled his eyes...

Chapter 12

Guo Long collapsed.

He collapsed in the hands of Qiao La.

The sight was caught by someone hiding behind a tree.

Who?

Zha Geli!

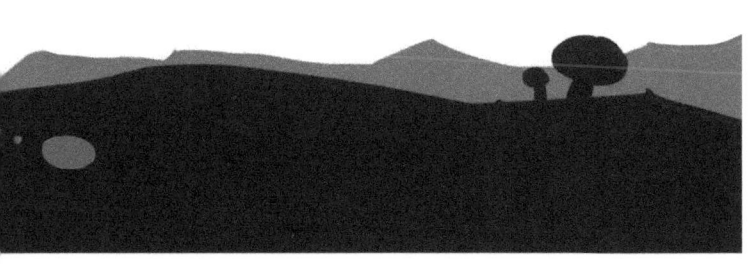

He had been shadowing Qiao La after parting company with Grandpa Du Ba.

Hiding in the dark, he saw Qiao La handing the charcoal to Wo Guli; he saw Wo Guli sending Qiao La to tell Duo Piao to issue his order by way of beating the drum; and saw Wo Guli dispatching Pi Luo to Galuo Village to ascertain the truth of the message conveyed by the charcoal.

Of course, Zha Geli had not expected that Qiao La, who was going to bring the order to Duo Piao, would be a lethal threat to the bandit-luring plan.

Therefore, Zha Geli had decided to let Qiao La go and follow Pi Luo when both of them set off at the same time.

He wanted to find out who the "old friend" was that Pi Luo was going to contact in the village.

He saw Pi Luo coming out of the shed dressed in the ethnic Blang costumes.

"Look out on your way!" advised Wo Guli.

Pi Luo stuff a handgun in his bosom and said, "Chief, wait for my signal tomorrow morning!"

Pi Luo set out.

Zha Geli trailed him.

Pi Luo went on a path leading out of the forest.

Zha Geli decided to pick anther route to outstrip him. He planned to get to the village ahead of Pi Luo and wait for him at the entrance of the village.

He quickly veered to another path. He was trotting furtively when suddenly he heard footsteps coming toward him.

Thump, thump, thump…

Zha Geli pulled out his handgun, moved the bushes apart with the muzzle, and looked. What?

The man who was walking over was none other than Qiao La!

Hasn't he gone to notify Duo Piao of Wo Guli's demand for issuing his order by beating the drum?

Before he had time to find an answer, Zha Geli saw something more alarming:

Qiao La suddenly dashed out from behind a tree and put his hands around someone's neck…

Who's the other person?

It's Guo Long!

Why is he here?

Zha Geli had no time to think. He dashed out of the bushes.

Whoosh!

Qiao La heard a gust of wind behind him.

It was too late for him to turn around. A second sound followed the first closely…

It was muffled and yet earthshaking.

It was the sound of a metal striking the back of his skull.

Qiao La blacked out and let go of Guo Long's neck.

Thud!

He dropped to the ground.

Zha Geli had knocked Qiao La to the ground with the grip of his handgun. He scooped Guo Long up in his arms.

Guo Long's lips were bluish purple, his eyes closely shut, and his face was ghastly pale.

Holding him in his arms, Zha Geli gave him mouth-to-mouth resuscitation.

Gradually, Guo Long's face warmed up, and he began to breathe through his flaring nostrils.

"Guo Long! Guo Long!"

Ah, who's calling me?

It sounds so familiar!

So far away...

And so close...

Suddenly, Guo Long felt it was raining.

Chilling raindrops dripped onto his face.

Guo Long opened his eyes.

He saw a face against the background of lush foliage.

Beams of sweat were dropping from it.

Good heavens! Is this for real?

"Uncle Zha Geli...!"

Guo Long cried out, his eyes blurred by swelling tears.

"Guo Long! Good boy..."

Zha Geli held Guo Long tight in his arms.

In his arms, Guo Long huddled like a little lamb.

Zha Geli felt his heartstrings tugged, feeling as if he were holding his own son.

It was true that he had been holding his son like this before he left home.

He bent his head down and pressed his cheek on Guo Long's.

"Son, tell me how you ended up here?"

Guo Long related to Zha Geli everything that had happened to him.

Now Zha Geli realized that the situation was more complicated than he had

Just then, Qiao La stirred and then started moaning.

Guo Long said, "He's not dead!"

Zha Geli responded, "I didn't mean to kill him."

Rustling, rustling, and rustling. It was Pi Luo who was coming over on a path not far away.

Zha Geli said, "Now, it's the most critical to trick them into beating the wooden drum. As long as the drum rolls, the bandits will gather together. Qiao La is as cunning as an old leopard, so I'll deal with him!"

Guo Long asked, "What about me?"

Zha Geli told him, "Pi Luo's hurrying to Galuo Village. He'll travel along this path all the way to it. Follow him closely, but make sure you never alert him. When the drumming started, I'll catch up with you. If…" Zha Geli paused, "If I fail to do so, you'll trail him to the village and find out whom he is going to contact. Then, go to see Company Commander Qi quickly. He knows what to do next!"

"Okay!" responded Guo Long as he fixed his eyes on Pi Luo. He was about to set off when Zha Geli stopped him by tugging his shirt.

Zha Geli asked, "What would you do if by chance you lose track of him?"

Guo Long blinked his eyes, "I'll go straight to Galuo Village to see Company Commander Qi!"

"That's right," nodded Zha Geli.

"What if Company Commander Qi were not available immediately?"

"Then...," Zhe Geli thought a little while and continued, "Go to Uncle Yue Mo. He's the deputy leader of the army-civilian joint defense team. He also knows what to do."

During their conversation, Pi Luo had passed by on the path.

Guo Long said, "I've got to go!"

"Good!" Zha Geli produced from his bosom the secret letter in the form of a bamboo strip that hunchbacked La Bendu had meant to deliver to Wo Guli. Handing it to Guo Long, he said, "Give this to Company Commander Qi or Uncle Yue Mo. Tell them there's a mole in the village and ask them to be on alert!"

Guo Long nodded. Stowing the secret letter away, he turned and left.

Watching his small, thin figure disappearing in the forest, Zha Geli suddenly felt that he still had a lot to say to him.

But Guo Long had vanished.

All had happened so quickly—running into each other and hurriedly parting company.

It was like a dream but not a dream.

It was not a dream but like a dream.

At this moment, silence reigned in the dense forest.

"Aw…!"

Qiao La opened his eyes moaning.

Why! It's already daybreak?

Qiao La saw a flash of white light in front of his eyes like a morning's ray shining through the thick foliage.

But he immediately saw clearly that it was the glint and flash of a knife instead of morning's ray.

The point of a sharp knife was pointed to the point between his eyebrows.

"Ah!"

Qiao La gave a shudder and intuitively attempted to put up a fight. But Zha Geli pinned him to the ground by pressing him on the chest.

"Don't move!"

Forcing a big smile on his face, Qiao La said, "…Bro, please be lenient!"

"If I hadn't been lenient, could you open your eyes?"

"May I ask which band do you belong in, bro?"

"Which band?" chuckled Zha Geli coldly, "If it were not for me, you would have found nothing but wind in the hole of the Chinese honey locust tree!"

"Bro, you're from Galuo Village, right?"

"I'm going back to it, too!"

"We're in the same trench, but why are you blocking my way?"

"I want to ask you something!"

"What's it?"

"How did you lose the rifles?"

"What...?" Qiao La was dumbfounded.

"Did you borrow your guts from a leopard? How dared you lie to the chief?"

While saying so, Zha Geli widened his eyes and tugged Qiao La by his collar.

"Go! Let's go back with me to see the chief!"

Qiao La panicked. If his lie was exposed in the presence of Wo Guli, and if the chief learned about the truth as to how he had lost the rifles, then what end would he come to? Gutting me would be a mild punishment. Picking each of my ribs clean with a knife would not be a surprise.

But soon, his terror gave way to suspicion.

Who's this guy?

How did he know that I lost the rifles?

Since he already knew I lied to the chief, why didn't he step forward to expose me?

Who was the boy that had followed me?

Why did he attack me with the grip of his gun when I was trying to get rid of the boy...?

While thinking so, he changed his expression into a smile.

"Well, bro! We can talk things through. Just tell me what you want!"

Zha Geli unexpectedly widened his angry eyes, "I want nothing! Go, let's go and see Chief Wo Guli!"

What? He really means to drag me to the chief, doesn't he? No way!

Besides, I still don't know who he is yet. I can't go to see the chief like this!

He was uncertain. What shall I do?

In fact, Zha Geli had no intention whatsoever to see Wo Guli.

He was adopting a tactic for subduing Qiao La by attacking his Achilles' heel.

Aware of his fear to see Wo Guli about the loss of the rifles, he pretended to take him to the chieftain of the bandits in all seriousness. He did so in order for Qiao La to try to deal with him.

Qiao La's plan was obvious: Going to Duo Piao first with the excuse of passing Wo Guli's order. Of course, even though Duo Piao was dead, he still had Zhuang Tie to rely on. Once they met, they could gang up against this stranger two to one!

Zhuang Tie did not know Zha Geli and would be on Qiao La's side for certain.

At present, this was Qiao La's only option.

This was exactly the option that Zha Geli had expected Qiao La to choose.

By forcing Qiao La to see Wo Guli, he actually meant to see Zhuang Tie.

Did Zha Geli not think of Qiao La's possible alliance with Zhuang Tie?

Yes, he did.

But he had a winning plan.

At this moment, he was eager to let Qiao La lead him to Zhuang Tie.

Without his guidance, how could he locate Zhuang Tie's shack?

"Go, hurry up! It's getting late. After we see the chief, I've got to go back to Galuo Village!"

As Zha Geli pressed repeatedly, Qiao La to finally seized on an idea:

"Bro, I did lose the rifles and lie to the chief. I deserve capital punishment! I'm willing to go with you and confess to the chief. But...but... Bro, you had sent out the charcoal, and you also know that we'll attack Galuo Village tomorrow morning. I've got the chief's directive and must pass it on to the next level!"

As he said so, he produced Wo Guli's directive in the form of a bamboo strip from his bosom.

"You see! The chief etched five cuts, which means our people must gather at the edge of the forest just before dawn.[5]

---

[5] In ancient China, the period between 7:00pm and 5:00am the next day was divided into five watches. The five cuts on the bamboo strips represent the fifth watch, namely the time between 3:00am and 5:00am, which was the time before dawn.

If I fail to pass the directive to the person in charge, I would bungle the whole thing. Could you please allow me to pass it on before we go to see the chief?"

Zha Geli said, "I know that the chief demanded that you tell Duo Piao to beat the drum as a way of issuing his order to rally our fighters!"

"Well, eh…"

Qiao La panicked…

How did he know so much?

Forget it. I can't afford to be overcautious anyway!

As long as I see Zhuang Tie, we'll be able to tackle him together.

With this in mind, Qiao La said,

"Bro, how about going to see Duo Piao first?"

"This is exactly what I want you to do!' said Zha Geli to himself.

Zha Geli nodded, "Alright, passing the directive comes before your confession. Otherwise, we'll bungle the whole thing. That would be too much a responsibility for either of us to bear."

Qiao La' mind was now set at rest.

Patting the dust off his clothes, he smiled at Zha Geli.

But his murderous intent was lurking behind the smile!

Zha Geli was aware of his intent for certain.

He said, "You go first and I'll follow."

Then, he kept a step's distance from Qiao La.

The two went into the depth of the dense forest one after the other.

Each with something on his mind, they walked rapidly.

Qiao La was contemplating on how to tackle Zha Geli as he walked in a hurry,

Contemplating while walking, he became increasingly confident. He could not but feel contented.

"I say, bro, when we meet Duo Piao in a minute, how am I going to introduce you?"

Still trying to figure out who I am, eh? Said Zha Geli to himself.

"It's up to you. I'm familiar with both Duo Piao and Zhuang Tie." responded Zha Geli casually.

What?

Qian La felt what Zha Geli had said to be a walnut choking in his throat: He could neither cough it off nor swallow it down.

He even knows the name of Zhuang Tie?

Qiao La was stupefied and perplexed.

He was familiar with both Duo Piao and Zhuang Tie?

Then, how come I don't know him?

Besides, I've never heard Duo Piao and Zhuang Tie ever mentioning him!

Gosh! If they're acquaintances and if they blame me for lying to the chief, then they'll gang up against me two to one, and the one would be me...!

The more he thought about it, the more scared Qiao La felt.

But a wicked idea dawned upon him as they walked on.

"Hey, Bro, I remember seeing a teen a moment ago. Where's he now?"

Zha Geli forced a scornful laugh, "You almost strangled him to death!"

Qiao La said, "I tried to get rid of me because I found him shadowing me. Who's he?"

Zha Geli responded, "He's my son!"

"Your son?"

"We came out together. But we ran into a tiger, and it broke us up."

Qiao La widened his eyes, "Then where's he now?"

Zha Geli said to himself, "Okay, I'll give you another 'walnut' bait!"

"I sent him to the chief. I asked him to tell the chief that I would take you there later!"

What?!

Qiao La was struck dumfounded. *It means that the chief is now waiting for me to return and meet out his punishment!*

Seeing Qiao La falling silent, Zha Geli know that his 'walnut' choked him again. Now it was time to give him some 'water' to wash the 'walnut' down.

"Don't worry! When we see Duo Piao and Zhuang Tie, we may just as well tell them the truth. If they both speak good of you, I'll let you off the hook this time by smoothing things over for you when we see the chief."

"Thank you, thank you!" Qiao La gave in to Zha Geli's maneuver.

The two quickened their pace.

They walked and walked when Qiao La said, "We're almost there!"

Zha Geli stepped quickly forward and came close to Qiao La, "Where?"

Qiao La reached his hand out and pointed, "Over there!"

Sure enough, Zha Geli saw a shack half hidden in the dense forest not far away.

Zha Geli asked, "You didn't recognize the wrong one, did you?"

Qiao La grinned, "How can I? I wouldn't have veered off the route to it with my eyes closed!"

"Great! You've accomplished your mission!" said Zha Geli.

Qiao La felt Zha Geli "compliment" gruesome. It sounded to mean more than what was said.

Suddenly, he felt a sharp pain in his rib case. Then, he shuddered as if he were electrified. He stood stiff, with his eyes popping out and his mouth wide-open. But he could by no means utter a sound.

Zha Geli's violent stab went into Qiao La's side between the ribs.

Such a stabbing skill prevented the victim from being able to let out even a whimper.

Zha Geli had learned the skill from Uncle Yue Mo.

As the knife was not pulled out from Qiao La's body, not a drop of blood flew from the wound. He staggered back and forth a few steps and fell thumping to the ground like a wooden door pane.

Qiao La was dead.

But there was a lot he had not known.

A lot he had wanted to get to the bottom of.

But his time had run out.

He just died not knowing why.

He had just done something useful before his death:

He had led Zha Geli to the destination.

Zha Geli cast a glance at the shack hidden in the thicket and found no trace of being perturbed.

He stooped down, fished out in Qiao La's clothes, and found Wo Guli's bamboo-strip directive, as well as the bamboo tube of wine. He unplugged it and sprinkled the wine on Qiao La's mouth and chest before he drank a big mouthful.

He lifted Qiao La's top and covered it over the handle of the knife stuck in his side. Then, he carried his body over his shoulder, with the face upon his shoulder. Seeing that there was no loophole anymore, he intentionally shuffled as he waded through the grass toward the shack, rustling the grass under his feet.

He was about to reach the shack when a swarthy-faced man appeared from behind the door, dagger in hand.

From Guo Long's description, Zha Geli concluded that this was Zhuang Tie.

Zha Geli raised his voice, "Hi Brother Zhuang Tie! Excuse me, please let me in!"

Zha Geli's mention of his name in the greetings stunned Zhuang Tie. Before he had time to size up this stranger, Zhuang Tie involuntarily made way for Zha Geli.

As he was doing so, Zhuang Tie asked, "What's going on?"

"Well, as we're going to attack Galuo Village, Brother Qiao La drank a little too much and passed out."

"I see, I see!" As he let Zha Geli into the shack, Zhuang Tie blinked his eyes, trying to make out who the man on Zha Geli's shoulder was. A whiff of wine bouquet assailed his nostrils and made them flare as he sniffed greedily.

"Yes, there's no mistake. He's Qiao La. But who're you?"

"Well, you and I haven't met before!" Zhe Geli said, exhaling breaths of wine from his mouth, "You think I'm a stranger, right?"

As he said so, Zha Geli placed Qiao La down on his side facing the wall of the shack on a heap of grass, giving the impression that he was in a slumber after excessive drinking.

"Yes, just tell me your name, please," Zhuang Tie stared into Zha Geli's eyes.

Zha Geli wobbled, seemingly trying hard to remain sober. As he mumbled, he produced with his trembling hand Wo Guli's bamboo-strip directive from his bosom.

"You, you go ahead and issue the chief's order! We'll talk when you finish!"

Zhuang Tie took the bamboo strip with hesitation. But when he looked at it, sure enough, it was a genuine directive from the chief.

"Let our men gather at the edge of the forest during the fifth watch?" asked Zhuang Tie.

"Ha-ha-ha," Zha Geli burst into a hysterical laughter, thinking, "he really knows what he's supposed to do!"

It was the kind of laughter in drunkenness.

Zhuang Tie forced a smile on his face.

"You're right. We'll gather together before dawn! We'll attack Galuo Village! You know, we'll attack Mengda Village at the same time. Or our chief would not have allowed us to get as drunk as a fiddler, right?"

Aware of Zhuang Tie's lingering suspicion, Zha Geli faked a burp reeking with the odor of alcohol and said,

"Brother Zhuang Tie, a moment ago, Duo Piao took the teen messenger to our chief. Guess what, the teenager had a piece of charcoal in his shoe. You know, our chief had long been expecting it! He was so happy that he threw a party. You don't know me, right? You don't recognize me, right? But you know Qiao La, don't you? You also know Pi

Luo, right? Duo Piao has been your shack mate, and you know him better than all the others, don't you?"

Zhuang Tie responded, "Yes, yes! I know all of them. Well, why hasn't Duo Piao come back?"

Zha Geli waved his big hand, "Don't interrupt me. Listen and speak after I finish! When you finish, I'll speak again! Well, we started drinking one bowl after another and ended up with a binge. Duo Piao drank so much that he couldn't stand on his feet. The chief had meant to dispatch him to you. But he slept so soundly that even thunder peals couldn't have wakened him up. Pi Luo was also dead drunk. Only Qiao La and I were still sober. The chief had planned to send Qiao La to you with his directive about his order but worried that he might bungle things up on his way in case the alcohol he had consumed would kick in. Therefore, he asked me to accompany him. If he had not led me here, I would never have been able to find you. Well, don't you think so? It's really a close call. We nearly messed things up!"

As he babbled, Zha Geli belched again.

"You, Brother Zhuang Tie, go and issue the order! Tomorrow, we'll take Galuo Village...! Ha-ha-ha! Ha-ha-ha...!"

Thump!

Zha Geli collapsed by Qiao La's side, still mumbling. Gradually, he fell silent.

His performance was just about right.

Zhuang Tie ping-ponged his eyes back and forth between the two drunkards and the bamboo directive in his hand.

What Zha Geli said makes perfect sense.

The chief's directive is genuine.

Everything fell into place and convinced Zhuang Tie.

He paused a little. Then he carried the wooden drum out of the shack and laid it flat on the ground.

The drum went off. It sounded low and deep:

Bum, bum, bum, bum, bum, bum, and bum!

The drum rolled seven times at first.

Bum! Bum! Bum! Bum! Bum!

Then five more times.

In the quiet forest, the sound of the wooden drum reached far and wide.

Zha Geli wondered, "So the order is being issued like this by the drumbeats?"

Where are the bandits who hear the drumbeats hiding?

Can they all hear the drumming?

Suddenly, the sound of drumming came from not too far away a place.

Bum, bum, bum, bum, bum, bum, and bum!

Seven times in a row first.

Bum! Bum! Bum! Bum! Bum!

Five more afterwards.

Initially, Zha Geli thought it was the echo of Zhuang Tie's drumbeats.

But he soon figured out that it was not an echo. Instead, it was the sound of one drum after another, passing on Wo Guli's order...

Bum, bum, bum, bum, bum, bum, and bum!

Bum! Bum! Bum! Bum! Bum!

Bum, bum, bum, bum, bum, bum, and bum!

Bum! Bum! Bum! Bum! Bum!

The wooden drums were hard to enumerate.

Zha Geli came to the realization that Wo Guli's bandits were divided into small groups of two or three and bigger teams of eight or ten. They scattered in the endless Mengna Forest. The benefit of the deployment was twofold: easy to hide and convenient to keep on living. During normal days, they would act separately by the units or teams. When the need to act together arose, they would gather by listening to the drumbeats.

Duo Piao and Zhuang Tie was the first stop that initiated the drumming.

From here, the drumming was relayed from one unit or team to another.

This band of bandits were really difficult to deal with!

If the main force of the bandit-suppressing troops launched a mop-up operation in the forest, it would find it hard to trace them. Even if encounters occurred, the troops would suffer heavy casualties. Wiping them out was simply out of the question.

Now, the drum order to rally was being issued.

Tomorrow morning, crows' caws throughout the valley would proclaim the end to Wo Guli's band of bandits!

Zha Geli could not help feeling excited.

The relayed drumbeats spread farther and farther and seemingly rolled louder and louder.

Bum, bum, bum, bum, bum, bum, and bum!

Bum! Bum! Bum! Bum! Bum!

Each drumbeat tugged at Zha Geli's heartstrings.

Just then, Zhuang Tie returned to the shack holding the wooden drum.

Zha Geli hastily closed his eyes.

Zhuang Tie stood by the door, cast a glance into the shack, and trampled into it.

Zha Geli held the barrel of his gun tight in his hand.

Zhuang Tie must now be dispensed!

It could be imagined that it would be still so dark before dawn that no one could see his hand held out before his face. Besides, one or two absentees were inevitable. When the crows cawed, Wo Guli would by no means change his battle plan just because one or two of the bandits failed to show up.

Zha Geli planned to kill Zhuang Tie with the grip of his handgun and bury the two bodies.

After he finished, he would catch up with Guo Long.

Just then, Zhuang Tie came in carrying the wooden drum.

Facing away from Zha Geli, he putting wooden drum down...

Zha Geli was ready to attack...

Suddenly, Zhuang Tie held up the drumstick in his hand and swiped it down to hit Zha Geli on his head.

The strike was so abrupt that Zha Geli did not have the time to dodge.

Bam!

The drumstick fell upon his head with great force.

Zha Geli saw stars and blacked out...

Why did Zhuang Tie launch this vicious attack?

Because he saw blood...

...Qiao La's blood!

With the knife still in Qiao La's body, no blood should have flown from the wound.

But when Zha Geli carried him on the shoulder, walked to the shack, and put him down on the grass, the knife that had been caught in the flesh began to loosen.

The pent-up blood oozed out of the crack and dyed the dry grass beneath Qiao La red.

When he returned to the shack with the drum, he immediately noticed the blood under Qiao La's body.

This otherwise simpleton suddenly became extraordinarily calm and cunning.

Pretending to put down the wooden drum, he drew close to Zha Geli. Meanwhile, he had gotten the drumstick ready.

He could initiate a different, agreed-upon pattern of drumming to cancel the previous drum order. Then, he would go to Wo Guli to report what had happened.

Zha Geli, who thought to have clinched his success received a sudden blow from Zhuang Tie!

Chapter 13

While Zhuang Tie attacked Zha Geli by surprise, Guo Long was hot one Pi Luo's trail.

Shuffling, shuffling, and shuffling! Trudging on the thick fallen leaves, Pi Luo crossed over a small muddy puddle covered with animal paw prints.

The water in the puddle was dimly clear and glittered with its reflection.

Whisking, whisking, and whisking! Wading through thick weeds, Pi Luo went around a tall wild-loquat tree with a large cluster of boletus speciosus mushrooms growing under it.

Rustling, rustling, and rustling! Pulling luxuriant branches and leaves apart, Pi Luo went into a dense bamboo grove.

On the edge of the bamboo grove, there stood a big tree laden with purple fruit.

Guo Long immediately recognized it. It was a "death upon touch" (antiaris toxicaria tree) tree!

Pi Luo walked and walked and suddenly disappeared behind a tree.

Guo Long was focusing his eyes on the tree when he heard a stir behind him.

He thought of it as a small animal passing by. But when he turned around, alas! His eyes were met by Pi Luo's icy look!

Pi Luo immediately held him by his arms and pulled them to his back.

"You rascal! Why are you here instead of cooking in the tavern?"

Following the same train of thought, Guo Long responded, "I'm here to collect some mushrooms…"

Pi Luo snorted, "Collecting mushrooms? But why don't you have your basket with you?"

Guo Long hemmed and hawed.

Pi Luo pulled his gun out, clocked it, and dug its muzzle in the back of Guo Long's head.

"Don't beat around the bush! I'll count three. If you don't tell me the truth, I'll pop your head open!"

Guo Long remained silent.

"One!"

Pi Luo started counting.

Guo Long clamped his teeth.

Pi Luo wouldn't trust me whatever story I'm going to fob off on him.

"Two!"

There was only one count left.

Guo Long panicked.

What shall I do?

Am I going to die like this?

His hands were gripped behind him while a chilling gun dug in the back of his head.

Guo Long chose to die.

Of his loved ones in this world, his ada and ama had died, and miserably. The only person that he found hard to tear himself away was Grandpa Du Ba. He had saved his life and brought him up. Depending on each other for survival, the grandpa and grandson were inseparable.

Guo Long thought of Grandpa Du Ba. Poor, lonely Grandpa Du Ba!

He somehow felt a tingle in his nose.

He seemed to see slightly hunchbacked Grandpa Du Ba scooping him up like a dead little lamb with his trembling hands. Silent tears streamed from his eyes turned bloodshot by the passing of time and rolled down his bark-like dry face through the permanently intricate network of wrinkles. The tears dripped and dripped and wet his beard…

Guo Long seemed to hear the hoarse and lamenting voice of Grandpa Du Ba, like a fallen, sweat-soaked old horse that was lying panting miserably at the foot of a mountain that it would never be able to surmount:

"…grandson, grandson! Why did you have such a hard lot!"

Guo Long wanted to say, "Grandpa, don't be so sad about me…"

But he could not say it.

He sobbed.

He said in tears, "I'm here to collect mushrooms indeed…"

A sneer flitted over his face, Pi Luo said, "Okay, here's what you deserve by lying!"

With that, he pressed his finger on the trigger…

Just at the critical moment, a kick was launched and knocked Pi Luo's gun into the midair.

Immediately afterward, two men rushed over and got hold of Pi Luo from his left and right.

Guo Long took a close look. The man rushing out to save him was tall and swarthy. He was dressed in a faded green uniform. On his properly clad army cap glistened a red five-star emblem with a golden border!

Ah, are these bandit-suppressing PLA uncles?

Guo Long was about to call out with joy when suddenly three more PLA uncles came out of the thicket.

The one in the front had a broad face with bushy eyebrows. He asked as he walked up,

"What's going on, Squad Leader Wang?"

One of the PLA soldiers controlling Pi Luo responded,

"Platoon Leader Sir, Squad Leader Wang reports! This bandit was going to kill this boy. We caught him and seized a handgun!"

Before Squad Leader Wang's voice had died away, Pi Luo suddenly screamed,

"I'm not a bandit. I'm a good man!"

Upon hearing it, Guo Long was flushed with anxiety, "He's not a good man. He's a bandit from Wo Guli's band!"

"Child, he can't fool us!" The platoon leader went up and ran his hand over his cheek, "We're here to suppress Wo Guli and his fellow bandits!"

Pi Luo said, "I'm from the Wo Guli's band alright, but not everyone from it is a bandit, isn't he?"

What he said battled everyone.

As he said so, he produced a bamboo strip from his bosom and handed it to the platoon leader.

Everyone was surprised.

Pi Luo said, "I took the chance to escape them and am going to deliver a message to the bandit-suppressing troops!"

The platoon leader took the bamboo strip and read in a hushed voice, "Wo Guli is going to attack Galuo Village."

"Yes, they're going to attack Galuo Village," said Pi Luo with sincerity. "I can't bear to see the villagers being harmed!"

Gazing into Pi Luo's eyes, the platoon leader asked, "Then you're…"

Holding back his tears, Pi Luo responded, "I was forced to join the bandits. I wanted to run away a long time ago, but never had a chance. Today, I finally ran away!"

"Thank you, fellow!" The platoon leader stepped forward and held his hands tightly.

Guo Long was dumbfounded.

What's going on?

Unable to figure it out, he felt bewildered.

Just then, the platoon leader said to Pi Luo, "We are a dagger squad of the bandit-suppressing forces. We're on our way to Galuo Village, but we're lost in the old forest."

Pi Luo said, "I'll take you there!"

"Great! Thank you!" said the platoon leader.

Suddenly, pointing at Guo Long, Pi Luo said, "You want to know why I threatened him with my gun? I suspected that he worked for Wo Guli as a scout!"

"Really?" The platoon leader came up to Guo Long, "Child, what's your name?"

"Guo Long."

"Well, tell me, what are you doing here in the old forest?"

"I…"

Guo Long told himself that he had better tell the truth.

But when he noticed Pi Luo pricking up his ears, he stopped short. *No, if I must tell, I can't do it in Pi Luo's presence. I'll go to Galuo Village with him and tell Company Commander Qi when I see him.*

Having made up his mind, Guo Luo said, "I came to the old forest to collect mushrooms, but I got lost…"

"Nonsense! Why don't you have your basket with you if you're here to collect mushrooms?" shouted Pi Luo.

Rolling his eyes at him, Guo Long responded, "I ran into a wolf and lost it when I fled."

"You're fooling us!" Pi Luo snorted and stepped forward.

The platoon leader stopped Pi Luo with a wave of his hand. Putting a smile on his face, he said unhurriedly, "Child, don't be afraid. It wouldn't matter even if you came here as a scout. Just tell us everything, and we'll escort you back home!"

What he said reminded Guo Long of the secret bamboo-strip letter in his bosom. He felt his chest subconsciously.

Unexpectedly, the platoon leader noticed his move, stepped quickly forward, and grabbed Guo Long by his chest. He searched and found the letter.

The bamboo strip read, "Don't attack Galuo Village tomorrow morning."

"Isn't this the secret letter to the bandits? Why did you lie to us?"

Gosh, it's all a misunderstanding.

Guo Long did not know whether to cry or to laugh, "No, no! That's not…"

"What do you mean by 'that's not?'" The platoon leader glared at him, "Obviously it is. How can you say it's not?"

Pi Luo was stupefied as well.

What? This boy is really a scout working for Wo Guli and is going to deliver his letter?

What's in the letter?

Suspicious as he was, he leaned close to the platoon leader,

"You see, I'm right, aren't I? He's really a scout who's going to deliver a secret letter to Wo Guli."

As he was speaking, he looked sideways at the platoon leader's hand.

The platoon leader balled his hand into a fist to prevent him from peeping at the secret letter.

Pi Luo grinned with embarrassment.

The platoon leader also grinned at him.

Suddenly, the platoon leader shouted, "Take him away and chop his head off!"

Guo Long was taken aback.

They're going to behead me?

Pi Luo said, "Who dispatched him to send the letter? We haven't gotten a clear answer from him. Don't chop it yet!"

The platoon leader shot a glare at him and roared, "Chop him? Ha, we're going to kill you!"

His roar had just died down when Squad Leader Wang stepped forward and grasped Pi Luo by his collar. Lifting him off the ground like a lantern, he was ready to take Pi Luo away.

Pi Luo's face changed from purplish black to ghastly gray. He screamed at the top of his lungs, "Don't kill me! Don't kill me! I've got something important to tell someone in Galuo Village. I'm Wo Guli's most trusted man..."

Hearing this, Squad Leader Wang faltered.

The platoon leader widened his eyes, "Stop your nonsense! Chop his head off!"

As he said so, he tore open his uniform and flapped its front like a fan to cool him-self off.

Pi Luo was dragged away while he was wailing.

Guo Long was completely stupefied, not knowing what in the world was going on.

Then, he cast a glance at the platoon leader who was fanning himself with the front of his uniform.

And his glance started him so much that he barely cried out...

———

On the chest of the broad-faced platoon leader was a tattoo of a double-headed snake.

"Argh!"

A bloodcurdling cry came from somewhere from the forest.

It was followed by deadly silence.

Rustling, rustling, and rustling. Squad Leader Wang returned trampling the fallen leaves. Blood was still dripping from his knife.

Then, the "platoon leader" showed his true colors.

"Guo Long, you're scared, aren't you? Let me tell you the truth. I'm Wo Guli's sworn brother Long!'

Ah, Brother Long?

The escaped bandit chief Brother Long?

"Three years ago, Brother Wo Guli and I bickered and fell out. Then I led some people away and formed a separate faction. Now, we're almost routed, and only the few of us have survived. We have to bite the bullet and come to rejoin Brother Wo Guli. I don't think he'll reject us. The thing is we've gone our own ways for too long. So I don't know where he is. We'd been milling around in the forest before we ran into you. Go and take us to Wo Guli!"

Guo Long was stunned! Gosh! *I almost told them everything. If I had done so, I'd bungle up everything!*

Now, Pi Luo is dead, but I'm besieged by a pack of wolves.

What shall I do?

It may be better for Pi Luo to have died. At least one of the causes of future trouble has been removed.

It'll be alright as long as I can manage to get to Galuo Village before daybreak.

But how can I escape the wolves around me?

They've mistaken me for Wo Guli's scout and made me lead them to him. Fine, I'll take this opportunity and try to flee on my way!

Having made his decision, Guo Long pretended that he came to a realization, saying to Brother Long, "Your costume made me really believe you were..."

'Ha-ha-ha!" Brother Long interrupted Guo Long, "Without these shabby clothes, we wouldn't have been able to get away from Mount Manuo!" While speaking, he suddenly looked sullen, "The Red Han are the mountain wind while we're the trees on the mountain. Wind will always go away, but trees will stay and stand firm. Let's wait and see! Guo Long, go and take us to Wo Guli!"

"Okay," said Guo Long.

"Hey, chief," the "Squad Leader Wang" quickly put in, "We felt hungry long ago, so much so that our stomachs are touching our backbones. Now that we've got our guide, how about eating something before we move on?"

The other three bandits also called for food.

"Okay! Let's cook something and move on," said Brother Long. Looking around, he asked, "Where can we find water?"

Water?

Cooking?

Guo Long felt secretly fired up, saying promptly,

"Let's go, there's a puddle not far away from here. The water is crystal clear!"

"Let's go!" nodded Brother Long.

Guo Long took the five bandits to the path where he came from.

After a while, the came to the crystal clear puddle.

A bamboo rat failed to flee in time, and "Squad Leader Wang" caught it alive.

Brother Long grinned from ear to ear, "Ha, before our main dish is ready, we have our side dish available now to drink wine with."

An idea dawned upon Guo Long. He followed up with the topic of cooking by saying, "I saw the grassy ground over there overgrown with mushrooms. They're good ingredients for a bamboo rat dish!"

"Ha-ha-ha! Great! Make your move! Build a fire, get some mushrooms, we'll go and see my big brother in high spirits after we eat."

The bandits sprang into action.

Brother Long set up a caravan pot.

Guo Long said, "The branches on the grassy ground is too damp to burn." Pointing to the wild loquat tree in the near distance, he continued, "There're two crow nests on that tree. They can be used to kindle the fire. I'll go and get them."

Brother Long raised his head and looked. Sure enough, there were really two crow nests on the wild loquat tree.

Guo Long rushed over, climbed up the tree, and poked the two crow nests down.

When he returned carrying the dried-up twigs, the bamboo rat had been skinned and put in the pot to boil. A few bamboo tubes had been filled with rice and water.

Only the mushrooms were not ready. It needed thorough cleaning. Otherwise the dirt on them would hurt the teeth.

Handing the twigs to Brother Long, Guo Long went to help with cleaning the mushrooms.

Soon, fire was kindled. The flames licked the bottom of the pot gurgling with boiling water. The tantalizing aroma of the bamboo rat began to permeate the surrounding air.

Guo Long and one of the bandits pulled up the fronts of their tops and carried the cleaned mushrooms in the fronts. They poured them into the pot.

It was time to eat. White rice was removed broken bamboo tubes while the boiled mushroom bamboo rat tasted scrumptious.

Brother Long offered his corn wine to the bandits, who munched and drank around the fire pit to their hearts' content.

They were eating and drinking merrily when "Squad Leader Wang," who was flushed to the roots of his hair, sprang up abruptly. While trying to hide a bamboo tube of rice in his top, he screamed, "It's mine! It's mine! It's mine!"

Everyone was taken aback, thinking that he was having a drunken fit.

But "Squad Leader Wang" went to the other side of a tree carrying the bamboo tube of rice. There, he dug his head in the base of the tree with his bottom sticking up high. "It's mine! It's mine! Don't grab it from me! Don't grab it from me!"

Brother Long went over to him, pulled him up on his feet, and slapped him on his face, saying,

"Are you crazy?"

"Squad Leader Wang" suddenly raised his rice bamboo tube and hit Brother Long on his head. "How dare you slap me? How dare you?"

Brother Long had not expected that he would strike back. Whack! The tube hit right on his forehead. The piping hot rice spilled all over his face. Scalded and hurt, Brother Long hopped and jumped like a shrimp.

The bandits were all dumbfounded. How outrageous! He dared to hit the chief!

But Brother Long did not punish "Squad Leader Wang." Instead, he hopped a few times and suddenly saw a group of thumb-sized dwarfs dressed in red and green. Men and women, old and young, they crowded around him singing and dancing.

Brother Long screamed, "Beat it! Beat it! I'll trample all of you to death!"

While screaming, he suddenly placed his arms around a tree and started banging his head against it. As he bumped, he said, "I want to get married! I don't want to get married…!"

Meanwhile, the "Squad Leader Wang" was kneeling on the ground yelling at a big tree,

"I'm a pig! I'm a pig…!"

The spectacle took the other three bandits by surprise at first. Then, they burst into a loud guffaw.

Tee-hee, tee-hee!

"He-he-he!"

"Ha-ha-ha!"

They were guffawing and guffawing when one of the bandits broke into an outburst of weird laughter:

"He-he! Ha-ha! Tee-hee…! Tee-hee! Hee-haw! Hee-haw…!"

As he laughed weirdly, he grabbed himself by his ears, his face flushing like the flowers of the flame of the forest tree. Now, his laughter gave way to crows, barks, and oinks alternately. While mimicking the sound of pigs, he crawled about on the ground.

The other two bandits soon followed suit, one dancing incessantly whereas the other singing in a female falsetto.

The five bandits threw themselves into a complete mess.

It was because the poison of the mushrooms they had eaten were taking effect.

How could they know that pretending to get twigs from the crow nests, Guo Long had collected a cluster of boletus speciosus mushrooms.

He had noticed the poisonous mushrooms as they had passed by the place.

He had hidden the poisonous boletus speciosus mushrooms in the fronts of his top that he was lifting. Taking the opportunity of helping the bandits wash the mushrooms, he had mixed them in.

The effect worked faster after alcohol intake.

Therefore, before they fully enjoyed their food and drink, the five poisoned bandits were plunged into disarray.

While the bandits were "indulging" in their "performances," Guo Long took to his heels.

He was free!

He had to get to Galuo Village before dawn.

But, he had just come out of the bamboo grove when he suddenly stopped.

No, I can't run like this!

After vomiting and passing loose stool, the bandits could recover from mushroom poisoning.

When they come to, they'll definitely try to find their way out of the grove. Then, they'll probably run into the Wo Guli bandits.

Besides, Brother Long still has the secret letter. I can't let him ruin our bandit-suppres-sing plan!

I must kill each and every one of them while they're still insane.

But how to?

As soon as the question popped up, he barely cried out with excitement…

Ah, the "death upon touch" tree!

Guo Long had recognized it when they had passed it by. It was an antiaris toxicaria tree laden with purple berries.

If a wound gets in contact with its white sap, any living creature, be it a human being or an animal, will be doomed to die.

Cutting off a branch, he ran toward the place where the bandits were.

When he arrived at the puddle, the bandits were still being lunatic. Two of them were lying on the ground unconscious.

Brother Long was still holding the tree and banging his head against it, his forehead already mangled.

Guo Long thrusted the white-sap-dripping branch at his forehead. He saw the sap mingling with the blood in the wound. Before long, Brother Long became sluggish. He was banging his head increasingly slowly before his limps and then his entire body stiffened. Holding the tree tight, he looked as if he were fast asleep.

He was dead.

Soon afterward, another three bandits also succumbed to the poison of the "death upon touch" tree branch.

Guo Long was about to kill "Squad Leader Wang" when the latter unexpectedly sprang up and grabbed Guo Long.

"How dare you! Do you want to kill me?"

Guo Long struggled off and turned to run.

Dagger in hand, "Squad Leader Wang" sprang to run after him.

"Where're you running? See if you can run from me!"

Half sober and half insane, the thug could not run steadily.

But they were too close. With only a few strides, "Squad Leader Wang" was able to grab Guo Long by his top.

A piece was ripped off!

Freed from his grasp, Guo Long ran and hid behind a big tree.

"Squad Leader Wang" threw himself upon Guo Long but lost his balance. He bumped his head against the tree.

"Ouch!" he screamed with great pain.

Guo Long rushed from behind the tree and jabbed the poisonous branch into his open mouth.

"Squad Leader Wang" gave a bloodcurdling cry and pulled the branch out of his mouth.

Knowing that his death was inevitable, Guo Long took flight.

"Squad Leader Wang" did not run after him. Waving the branch in his hand, he shouted,

"Stop! Stop! Where're you running?"

His shouts suddenly changed into a laughter, which sounded like the hoot of an owl.

"Hoo hoo, hoot! Hoo hoo, hoot! Do you think I really killed Pi Luo? Let me tell you! He's not dead! I let him go! Hoo hoo, hoot! Hoo hoo, hoot! I set him free!"

His yelling declaration stunned Guo Long.

What? Pi Luo isn't dead!

Silence suddenly fell behind him.

Guo Long turned around, only to see…

"Squad Leader Wang" was lying on his back, with his limbs stretching out.

He died of blood coagulation.

But his terrifying laughter was still ringing in the gloomy forest.

Did he tell the truth?

If so, Pi Luo must have found his way out of the bamboo grove.

Guo Long felt as if he were on pins and needles.

He made straight to the edge of the grove. Running as fast as a flying hawk, he wished that he could get out of the grove and arrive at Galuo Village in one breath.

As he ran, he mumbled doubtingly:

Is it true that Pi Luo is still alive?

Chapter 14

Pi Luo was not dead indeed.

Before "Squad Leader Wang" dragged him to his execution, Brother Long had changed his mind. He secretly gestured "Squad Leader Wang" to let Pi Luo go.

Taking the hint, "Squad Leader Wang" hauled Pi Luo to the depth of the forest, made a slashing cut on his bottom, and released him.

Covering his bottom with his hands, Pi Luo took to his heels.

He got out of the forest before sunset and headed straight toward Galuo Village.

He trudged on the bumpy road like an aspiration in the moonlight.

While setting his mind on reaching his destination, he was unaware of someone following him closely.

Who was following him?

It was Zha Geli!

After being stricken down with a drumstick by Zhuang Tie, Zha Geli had not given the attacker a second chance. Grasping a handful of dirt from the floor, he cast it over Zhuang Tie's face to blind him. In a vicious fight that ensued immediately afterward, Zha Geli, master of martial arts, dealt Zhuang Tie a fatal blow.

After disposing of his and Qiao La's bodies, he tidied up the shed and rushed to the forest path to catch up with Guo Long.

He missed Guo Long but ran across Pi Luo who had just escaped from death.

Zha Geli did not alert him. He shadowed him.

Galuo Village was shrouded in the dimly bright moonlight.

Merged with the dark night, one stilt bamboo house after another appeared like rolling hills.

It must have been deliberately arranged by Company Commander Qi. The residents of almost all the bamboo houses had smothered the fire in their fire pits and gone to sleep in the dark as usual.

The whole village appeared natural, tranquil, and peaceful.

There was not the slightest hint that this was the eve of a fierce battle.

Indeed, gunshots would flare up at dawn in the valley, where Wo Guli's bandits would be encircled and suppressed. It was what the villagers had been hankering for over the years. How could the villagers have gone to sleep without the arrangement? They would have sat up chatting and laughing around their fire pits with flames leaping briskly. Young men and women could even have danced their cheerful ethnic Dongbacha dance.

But none of these were happening.

Everything was as usual.

This external appearance of usualness alone gave Pi Luo the impression that nothing particular had happened to Galuo Village.

It will belong to Wo Guli tomorrow!

Pi Luo sneaked into the village under the cover of the shadows of the Chinese windmill and areca palm trees.

Zha Geli followed was hot in pursuit.

Seeing the village in peaceful slumber, Zha Geli could not help admiring Uncle Yue Mo's ability.

There is no doubt that everything in this peaceful village had been arranged by Uncle Yue Mo in cooperation with Company Commander Qi.

In Zha Geli's eyes, Uncle Yue Mo, a veteran hunter, was composed, experienced, unequivocal in his stand, and well-versed in martial arts. When the army-civilian joint defense team had first been set up, Zha Geli had recommended Yue Mo to be the deputy team leader at the meeting. The loud cheers exhibited his popularity among the villagers.

Zha Geli followed Pi Luo closely as the latter navigated his way around one stilt bamboo house after another.

Who's he looking for?

Who's his "old friend?"

Under two tall Chinese windmill palm trees ahead, there sat a stilt bamboo house.

The bamboo door was ajar, revealing a brightly burning fire pit.

This was Zha Geli's home.

A cozy home!

With the door ajar, Na Sha was waiting for Zha Geli to return.

With the fire in the fire pit brisk, Na Sha was expecting Zha Geli to come home.

At the time, was Little Lige sleeping or waiting for his return while snuggling against his mother by the fire pit?

This morning, when he opened his eyes, he must have asked his ama if his ada had caught him a fire-tailed sunbird.

He must have been waiting for the whole day.

From sunrise to sunset.

But he had waited in vain.

But now, Little Lige did not know that his ada was just passing by the house.

Neither did Na Sha know that her husband was passing by the house.

…he was passing by quietly, quietly.

Zha Geli hoped that Na Sha could detect his familiar footsteps.

He wanted to tell Na Sha: I'm back. Don't worry anymore!

Zha Geli wished that his son's chubby face could pop out of the window.

He wanted to tell him: Now that I'm back, I'll catch you a fire-tailed sunbird!

But Zha Geli pussyfooted by his house without making the slightest stir.

He feared that his wife would hear his familiar footfalls.

He feared to see his son's chubby face popping out of the window.

He walked even quieter and faster like a fleeting meteor.

Pi Luo navigated his way around three more stilt bamboo houses.

He sneaked into a thick hardy banana grove and was

about to walk further when suddenly...

Whoosh!

...a man dashed out of a thicket and placed an arm around his neck.

Before Zha Geli could see clearly, Pi Luo had already been wrestled to the ground.

Pi Luo moaned and groaned.

His mouth was covered by a big hand. Then he was trussed up.

Zha Geli took a closer look, only to see Uncle Yue Mo! It was him who had captured Pi Luo!

He heard Uncle Yue Mo asking in a stern and yet hushed voice,

"What're you doing?"

"I...I'm a passer-by. I'm a good man..."

"A good man? But why do you have a gun?"

"..."

"Behave yourself! Come to the army-civilian joint defense team's office with me. If you don't behave, I'll skin you!"

Upon hearing this, Zha Geli came out of the shadow of a tree.

"Who is it?"

Uncle Yue Mo pointed his gun at him.

"Me!"

"Zha Geli?"

"Yes, it's me!"

"Oh, great! You're back finally. We've been expecting you!"

Zha Geli came up and cast a glare at Pi Luo.

"This thug came from Wo Guli. I've been shadowing him!"

"Really?" Uncle Yue Mo fixed him with a surprised stare, "What's he here for?"

Zha Geli said, "It's a long story. Let's go. I'll tell you when we get to the joint-defense office."

As he said so, he stepped forward and grabbed Pi Luo by his collar.

Pi Luo wiggled in resistance.

Just then, Zha Geli suddenly felt a stab of pain on the side, as if a needle were thrusted into his rib case.

It was not a needle. It was a knife!

A sharp knife!

The knife was driven into the side of his chest through the ribs.

Its tip penetrated his heart!

Such a stab prevented the victim from crying out.

Zha Geli was having the same experience.

He reached his trembling hand to his chest...

In his memory, there was only one person who could stab people with such a technique in Galuo Village.

It was Uncle Yue Mo!

It was him who passed the technique to one person. That was Zha Geli himself.

It was him who...?

No, he can't...

Zha Geli turned around...

In the chilling moonlight, Yue Mo fixed his wide-open

eyes at Zha Geli, who was trembling with agony.

Yue Mo's face was as chilling as iron.

A piece of ore!

Yue Mo taught Zha Geli this stabbing skill.

And he took Zha Geli's life with it so he was dying in silence!

Suddenly, Zha Geli began to know and understood a lot!

But his knowledge and understanding came too late.

A wary man and an Aini man as brave as a tiger, coll-apsed.

He fell after he turned around.

Not only did he see his enemy, but he also saw his own home under the Chinese windmill palms.

A house with the door ajar…

With the flames in the fire pit burning brilliantly…

Zha Geli closed his eyes slowly.

In front of his eyes, the firelight of the fire pit turned into a red flash, a gigantic fire-tailed sunbird!

After killing Zha Geli, Yue Mo untied Pi Luo imme-diately.

"Old friend…" Pi Luo was trying to say something but was stopped.

"Be quiet! Quick, let's carry him away."

"To where?"

"To my pigsty. We'll dig a pit and bury him in it!"

Pi Luo stooped down and lifted Zha Geli by his arms.

He had things on his mind and could not help mumbling:

"At the fifth watch…"

Chapter 15

It was the fifth watch, or, immediately before dawn.

The Longba Gate of Galuo Village was covered in the morning fog.

Nude sculptures of a man and a woman, idols of fertility, flanked the gate.

A man rushed out of the dense fog carrying a bamboo tube and charged toward the Longba Gate.

Splash! He poured the content out of the bamboo tube onto the gate.

A pungent odor immediately permeated the dense fog.

It was not water!

It was kerosene.

Before he struck a match, four big hands grabbed the man and pressed him to the ground.

"Ah!"

With a cry of alarm, the man plopped to the ground.

Soon, he heard a familiar voice:

"Uncle Qi, he's Pi Luo!"

Without turning to look, Pi Luo could tell from the voice that it was Guo Long.

He was right! It was Guo Long indeed!

Guo Long had managed to get back to Galuo Village and found Company Comman-der Qi.

"Pi Luo, we've been waiting for you for a long time!" said Company Commander Qi, "Who's your old friend?"

Pi Luo rolled his eyes and clammed up.

Just then...

Bang!

A ringing gunshot broke the morning silence and resonated in the valley.

The crows on the big banyan tree in front of the village were startled and thrown into disarray.

Caw! Caw! Caw!

Caw! Caw! Caw!

Caw! Caw! Caw!

The caws of such a large flock of crows were deafening and far-reaching.

Thousands of flapping and fluttering wings pierced the fog and clouds and blocked a large part of the sky.

With the caws of the flying crows, heavy gunfire was heard coming from the valley of Mount Beilu.

The battle to annihilate the Wo Guli bandits began!

Holding Company Commander Qi by his hand, Guo Long jumped with joy and shouted at the startled crows:

"Caw, crows! Fly, crows! The Wo Guli bandits are done for!"

Tears swelling in his eyes, Company Commander Qi said, "This day hasn't come easily!"

Reports of guns and hand grenades resonated in the valley.

Looking up at the crows in the sky, the people by the Longba Gate were overwhelmed with the joy of triumph.

But none noticed that the trussed-up Pi Luo, who was sitting limply on the ground, had hit the ground head first.

An arrow was stuck on his back!

Just then, Yue Mo walked over from the direction of the banyan tree.

From a distance, he shouted, "Company Commander Qi, can you hear how concentrated the gunfire is?"

Grandpa Du Ba, who was following him, said with excitement, "The gunfire sounds like burning bamboo!"

Looking around with knitted eyebrows, Company Commander Qi said, "The battle has begun, but our Zha Geli hasn't returned yet!"

Holding Grandpa Du Ba and Company Commander Qi by their hands, Guo Long shook them as he said, "Don't worry! Uncle Zha Geli is a super hero, and he will be back for sure!"

Yue Mo said, "Yes, Zha Geli will be back. He is indeed the hero of our Galuo Village!"

First written in September of 1981 in Beijing
Revised in April 29, 2018